PENGUIN SWADESH

Increase Your WORD POWER

Prof. Y. K. Modi is a distinguished language teacher and writer. His book *Modern Letter Writing* is also available in Hind Pocket Books.

AF530416

Increase Your WORD POWER

PROF. Y.K. MODI

PENGUIN
SWADESH

An imprint of Penguin Random House

PENGUIN SWADESH

USA | Canada | UK | Ireland | Australia
New Zealand | India | South Africa | China | Singapore

Penguin Swadesh is part of the Penguin Random House group of companies whose addresses can be found at global.penguinrandomhouse.com

Published by Penguin Random House India Pvt. Ltd
4th Floor, Capital Tower 1, MG Road,
Gurugram 122 002, Haryana, India

Penguin Random House India

First published in Hind Pocket Books by Penguin Random House India 2019
This edition published in Penguin Swadesh by Penguin Random House India 2024

Copyright © Penguin Swadesh 2001

All rights reserved

10 9 8 7 6 5 4 3 2

The views and opinions expressed in this book are the author's own and the facts are as reported by him which have been verified to the extent possible, and the publishers are not in any way liable for the same

ISBN 9789353492427

Printed at Repro India Limited

This book is sold subject to the condition that it shall not, by way of trade or otherwise, be lent, resold, hired out, or otherwise circulated without the publisher's prior consent in any form of binding or cover other than that in which it is published and without a similar condition including this condition being imposed on the subsequent purchaser.

www.penguin.co.in

FSC www.fsc.org MIX Paper from responsible sources FSC® C047271

This is a legitimate digitally printed version of the book and therefore might not have certain extra finishing on the cover.

PREFACE

In the beginning was the word, and the word was with God, and the word was God. —The Bible

Words are *mantras.* There is magic in words. There is power in the words. There is magnificence in the words. The more words you know and can use properly, the more power you have.

Little wonder, the greatest sermons of the world in the Bible, the Vedas, and other religious books are delivered in the simplest words. What could be a simpler word than *Om* ? Yet, it is a most powerful word.

Every word is a key to the universe. It has the potentialities of OM. The more words you know, the more keys you hold to the secret treasures and pleasures of this world and the worlds beyond.

Jane Austen and the Bronte sisters were poorer to the extent that they did not know that *batatawada* came from Bombay and not from Boston; and that they had no opportunities to see movies which did not exist in their times. Now films, television, newspapers and journals and the internet all help you to enrich your vocabulary. You have to choose a few golden grains from the chaff. As our savant C. V. Raman said, "You may find a diamond in a ploughed field, but you will not recognise it unless you are a jeweller."

The purpose of this book is to give you expertise and the knowhow of recognising diamonds when you come across them in the ploughed fields of journalism and everyday life. If you do not recognise jewels; you can hardly appreciate them. This book would help you in your quest.

Today, good writing can only be appreciated by a minority. The majority is just not interested. Few folk care to write well, and fewer still care to read well. But great writing is its own reward. It ennobles the writer and sublimates the environment.

From the magic of words to the magic of life is but one step.

CONTENTS

CHAPTER I	The Choice of Words	*1*
CHAPTER II	Quintessential Grammer	*6*
CHAPTER III	Grammatic Transformation	*14*
CHAPTER IV	Words	*27*
CHAPTER V	Word Forms	*63*
CHAPTER VI	Definitions	*71*
CHAPTER VII	One-Word Substitutes	*80*
CHAPTER VIII	Ideas Make Words	*91*
CHAPTER IX	Idioms	*100*
CHAPTER X	Idiomatic Phrases	*109*
CHAPTER XI	Words From the Newspapers	*135*
CHAPTER XII	Spellings	*142*
CHAPTER XIII	Synonyms and Antonyms	*148*
CHAPTER XIV	Homonyms	*152*

CHAPTER XV	Rhyming Words	*157*
CHAPTER XVI	Foreign Phrases	*160*
CHAPTER XVII	Word-Building Exercises 1	*164*
CHAPTER XVIII	Word-Building Exercises 2	*166*

Other books in this series

1. *Eric Watson*
   The Art of Conversation

2. *Eric Watson*
   Correct Manners and Etiqutte

3. *Eric Watson*
   Idioms and Phrases

4. *Sunil Upadhyaya*
   Happiness the Key to Success & a Full Life

CHAPTER I

The Choice of Words

It is not the number of words you know that matters. Quality is more important than quantity. You have to find the right word at the right time. That is a hard road you have to follow and you should be ready to follow, because it is richly rewarding.

The great writers like Tennyson and Stevenson, Shelley and Keats, quite often spent long hours to select the right word to express their ideas. A big word is easy to pick and choose; but a right, simple word is often elusive and difficult to come by. Winston Churchill, one of the greatest Prime Ministers of England, and Abraham Lincoln, one of the greatest Presidents of America, quite often spent long days and nights over their historic speeches. Lincoln's Gettysberg Address and Churchill's blood-toil-sweat-and-tears speech were born that way. Today these utterances, couched in the simplest of words, are masterpieces of English literature.

Simplicity is Most Sublime

Believe it or not, simplicity is the most sublime. Anybody can gather large multisyllabic words but to express the greatest ideas in the simplest words requires a special technique, which is not always easy.

The greatest books and writings of the world are the simplest. Look at the Bible, for instance. It conveys its ideas with such remarkable simplicity, that its style is inimitable:

"Blessed are the poor, for they shall see God."

"Know ye the truth, and truth shall make thee free."

"To him who hath shall be given; and he who hath not from him will be taken away even what he hath."

"A camel can pass through the eye of a needle but a rich man cannot enter heaven."

Study Shakespeare and you will find that the greatest Shakespearean ideas are conveyed in the simplest words:

"To be or not to be—that is the question."

"Uneasy lies the head that wears the crown."

"There is nothing good or bad but thinking makes it so."

"Mercy is doubly blessed. It blesses him who gives and him who takes."

Study the style of Mahatma Gandhi and you will find his statements, couched in the simplest words, are the most powerful :

"Defeat has no place in the dictionary of non-violence."

"Hatred ever kills, love never dies."

"Strength of numbers is the delight of the timid.

"The valiant of spirit glory in fighting alone."

"I shall rather have violence than cowardice masquerading as non-violence."

"Whatever you do, be true to yourselves and to the world."

Two Kinds of Words

There are two kinds of words:

I. Common practical words.

II. Technical and professional words.

You have to be careful about the choice of common practical words because quite often you have no choice in the determination of technical and professional words.

Every science has its own terminology and those who study science have to learn the technical terms of that science to make the subject understandable. Every technical word is the growth of long experience and research and tells a lot in a phrase or two. For example,

"Bright's Disease" means little to an ordinary reader, beyond fever and pain in the body; but the doctor who spent his life in the research of "Parkinson's disease" also died of Parkinson's disease! To a doctor, much clinical research and experience is concealed in the phrase. Similarly, researches and experiments in science are named after the great scientists who have invested years in them.

H_2O means nothing to a lay person but to a scientist it means water. An ordinary person who wants to use a different word for water may call it *aqua pura.* It means pure water in Latin.

"Will you have Coke?"

"No, I will prefer *aqua pura.*"

Sounds quite funny. So let water be water.

Learn Great Words from Great Writers

Memorize great quotations from great men and women and these will help you to cultivate your style and the use of simple words in great style. By memorizing great quotations, the use of the right words at the right spot will become habitual for you.

A thing of beauty is a joy forever. — *Keats*

Child is the father of man. — *Wordsworth*

Not gold but only men can make a nation great and strong. — *Emerson*

The machinery of labour strikes down the labourer.
— *Karl Marx*

The only thing you have to fear is fear itself.

— President Roosevelt

Man is a political animal *— Aristotle*

There is a destiny that shapes our ends, rough hew them how we will. *— Shakespeare*

Lack of money is the root of all evil.

— G.B. Shaw

Power corrupts. Power always corrupts. Absolute power corrupts absolutely. *— Lord Acton*

The reactionaries have been winning the battles and losing the war. *— Walter Lipmann*

He can who thinks he can. *— Anonymous*

Never take anything for granted.

—Benjamin Disraei

CHAPTER II

Quintessential Grammar

Everything written or spoken is made up of sentences. A sentence is made of words. Words are classified into eight different groups.

1. Noun

A noun is the name of a person, animal, place or thing. Nouns are naming words.

Example: Jaggi, cat, Amritsar, room, inkpot, etc.

2. Verb

A verb is a word which describes what is done. It denotes action.

Example: go, come, sleep, wake up, stand, etc.

3. Pronoun

A pronoun is a word which takes the place of a noun.

Example: I, you, he, she, they, it, them, etc.

4. Adjective

An adjective is a word which qualifies a noun. Adjectives are picture-words as they create a certain picture in the mind.

Example: Good, bad, strong, ugly, beautiful, dark, etc.

5. Adverb

An adverb is a word which modifies a verb. Adverbs are verb helpers.

Example: Slowly, wisely, quickly, gently, here, these, now, yesterday.

6. Preposition

A preposition is a word which is placed before a noun or a pronoun to show its relation to some other noun or pronoun.

Example: In, out, of, above, below, into, with, etc.

7. Conjunction

A conjunction is a word which joins two words or two sentences together. Conjunctions are link-words.

Example: And, but, or, etc.

8. Interjection

An interjection is a word which expresses surprise, sorrow, pain, etc.

Example: Oh! ah! alas! hurrah! cheerio!, etc.

Kinds of Nouns

There are five kinds of nouns:

1. *Proper Noun*: It is the name of a particular person, place or thing: Ram Singh, Mumbai, Ganges, Himalayas, etc.
2. *Common Noun*: It is the name of several persons, places, species or things: house, city, school, dog, country.
3. *Material Noun*: It is the name of a substance: water, iron, copper, etc.
4. *Collective Noun*: It is the name of a group of things taken together: army, library, team, chain, etc.
5. *Abstract Noun*: Shows quality: strength, bravery, goodness, evil, virtue, whiteness, etc.

Collective Nouns

A library of books.	A series of events.
A bale of cotton.	A set of tools.
A board of directors.	A shower of rain.
A cluster of stars.	A shoal of fish.
A bunch of keys.	A suit of clothes.
A bouquet of flowers.	A swarm of flies.

A litter of pups.

A pack of hounds.

A crowd of people.

A hive of bees.

A chain of mountains.

A class of students.

A fleet of ships.

A string of camels.

A team of horses.

A tuft of grass.

A volley of shots.

A tribe of people.

A bundle of sticks.

Genders

There are four kinds of genders:

All males form the *Masculine Gender*: horse, lion, king, lord, etc.

Females are part of the *Feminine Gender*: mother, woman, hen, etc.

Common Gender can be either male or female: child, friend, person, enemy, animal, etc.

Neuter Gender is something without gender : stone, rock, desk, chair, book, etc.

Masculine	*Feminine*	*Masculine*	*Feminine*
Nephew	Niece	Duke	Duchess
Bachelor	Maid	Waiter	Waitress
Earl	Countess	Hunter	Huntress
Sir	Madam	Host	Hostess
Washerman	Washerwoman	Bull	Cow

Stag	Hind	Bull-calf	Cow-calf
Author	Authoress	Peacock	Peahen
Shepherd	Shepherdess	Heir	Heiress
Man-servant	Maid-servant	Landlord	Landlady
Actor	Actress	Buck	Doe

Names of Young Creatures

Parent	*Young*	*Parent*	*Young*
Mother	Child	Swan	Cygnet
Cow	Calf	Deer	Fawn
Hen	Chicken	Cat	Kitten
Goose	Gosling	Dog	Pup
Horse	Foal		

Numbers

One thing is a Singular Number. Two or more things are called Plural Numbers.

Singular	*Plural*	*Singular*	*Plural*
Book	Books	Man	Men
Egg	Eggs	Woman	Women
Key	Keys	Mouse	Mice
Fly	Flies	Louse	Lice
Lady	Ladies	Tooth	Teeth
Knife	Knives	Ox	Oxen

Thief	Thieves	Child	Children
Buffalo	Buffaloes	Analysis	Analyses
Potato	Potatoes	Axis	Axes
Bamboo	Bamboos	Crisis	Crises
Portfolio	Portfolios	Basis	Bases
Phenomenon	Phenomena	Wolf	Wolves
Leaf	Leaves	Genus	Genera
Shelf	Shelves	Erratum	Errata
Dwarf	Dwarfs	Stratum	Strata
Proof	Proofs	Focus	Focii
Nucleus	Nuclie	Radius	Radii
Scarf	Scarfs or Scarves	Whart	Wharfs or wharves

Plurals only

Some nouns are used in plural form only:

Alms—annals—billiards—breeches—braces—compasses—eatables—measles—moveables—pincers—premises—proceeds—riches—scissors—spectacles—thanks—tongs—trousers.

Articles

Articles are not a separate part of speech. They are as good as adjectives.

A, An and *The* are the three articles.

Articles become articulated when they are put in proper places. *A* and *An* are Indefinite Articles, because they denote any one person, place or thing; while *The* is a Definite Article, because it indicates a particular person, place or thing.

An is used when a word begins with a vowel. "A", "E", "I", "O", and "U" are vowels. "H" and "Y" are also articulated as vowels when they are silent.

For example: '*An* apple, *an* inkpot, *an* ovaltine drink, *an* heir, *an* honourable gentleman, *an* hour, etc.'

A is used with all singular common nouns beginning with a consonant, a word which does not begin with a vowel, that means all nouns which do not begin with A, E, I, O and U.

A and *An* are used with a proper noun which has the force of a common noun, such as :

'Ritu is *a* Lata Mangeshkar.'

The is used with the names of rivers, oceans, mountain ranges, certain states, etc.:

Chandigarh is *the* capital of the Punjab.

The source of *the* Ganges is in *the* Himalayas.

The is also used with the names of books and newspapers: "*The* Bible", "*The* Hindustan Times", "*The* Koran", etc.

The used with adjectives converts them into plural

nouns: "*The* Indians", "*The* virtuous conquer," "*The* wicked."

No article is used before Abstract Nouns, Material Nouns and Plural Nouns,

"Truth triumphs."

"Diamonds are Coal."

"Pathans are good fighters."

CHAPTER III

Grammatic Transformations

Unknown words can be created grammatically out of the known words. A noun can be made into a verb or a verb can be converted into a noun, adverb or adjective by following well-established grammatic techniques. An understanding of these rules and regulations can be highly challenging as well as rewarding. You acquire improved comprehension and an increased confidence. Practical experience enables you to deal with all kinds of situations. Grammatical forms demonstrate the diversity and richness of the English language.

Adjectives

1. *"Y" for adjectives*

Fur	Furry	Salt	Salty

Cat	Catty	Fault	Faulty
Leak	Leaky	Dirt	Dirty

2. "Ish" for adjectives

Self	Selfish	Grey	Greyish
Sweet	Sweetish	Skit	Skittish
Red	Reddish	Wasp	Waspish

3. "Ish" with adjective

   When a word is already an adjective in form, by adding "ish", it gives the sense of "a little."

Red	Reddish (a little red)	Big	Biggish (a little big)
Sweet	Sweetish (a little sweet)	Cold	Coldish (a little cold)

4. "Ed" changes a verb into an adjective

Love	Loved	Water	Watered
Finish	Finished	Spirit	Spirited

5. "Ian" or "an" makes an adjective or a noun with the sense "belonging to"

India	Indian	Belgium	Belgian
Russia	Russian	Germany	German
America	American	Australia	Australian

6. "Ese" also makes adjective with the sense of "belonging to"

China	Chinese	Vietnam	Vietnamese

Japan	Japanese	Sudan	Sudanese

7. “Ul” and “Al” make adjectives, meaning “relating to”

Senses	Sensual	Hormone	Hormonal
Spirit	Spiritual	Autumn	Autumnal
Intellect	Intellectual	Rite	Ritual

8. “En” makes an adjective, meaning “Made of”

Wood	Wooden	Oak	Oaken
Silk	Silken	Gold	Golden
Lead	Leaden		

9. “Ic” makes an adjective, meaning “of the nature of”

Acid	Acidic	Majesty	Majestic
Metal	Metallic	Prose	Prosaic
Hero	Heroic	Poet	Poetic

10. “Ous,” “ious,” make adjectives, meaning “having”

Grace	Gracious	Mystery	Mysterious
Nerve	Nervous	Space	Spacious
Malice	Malicious	Fallacy	Fallacious

11. “Ive” makes an adjective, meaning “causing”

Abuse	Abusive	Accumulate	Accumulative
Exhaust	Exhaustive	Relate	Relative

12. “Hyper” means “over, above, excessive”

Sensitive	Hypersensitive	Critical	Hypercritical
Somnia	Hypersomnia	Active	Hyperactive
Dimensional	Hyperdimensional		

Noun

13. "Er" changes verb into noun with "doer" sense

Write	Writer	Catch	Catcher
Kill	Killer	Lose	Loser
Mill	Miller	Gain	Gainer

14. "Ness" turns an adjective or adverb into noun

Careful	Carefulness	Swiftly	Swiftness
Careless	Carelessness	Timeless	Timelessness
Callous	Callousness	Timely	Timeliness
Slowly	Slowness	Reasonable	Reasonableness

15. "Ability" makes noun from "able"

Capable	Capability	Breakable	Breakability
Feasable	Feasability	Workable	Workability

16. "Ite" makes a noun meaning "native of"

Urban	Urbanite	Suburban	Suburbanite
Delhi	Delhite	Favour	Favourite

17. "ion or tion" turn a verb into a noun

Act	Action	Form	Formation
Affect	Affection	Locate	Location
Dictate	Dictation	Reflect	Reflection

18. "Age" makes a noun

Carry	Carriage	Rough	Roughage
Marry	Marriage	Store	Storage

19. "Ment" makes a noun, meaning "state of"

Content	Contentment	Improve	Improvement
Disillusion	Disillusionment	Attain	Attainment
Align	Alignment	Enlighten	Enlightenment

20. "Ery" makes an abstract noun, showing quality

Brave	Bravery	Bake	Bakery
Witch	Witchery		

21. "Ity" makes an abstract noun, showing quality

Absurd	Absurdity	Able	Ability
Human	Humanity	Disable	Disability
Capable	Capability		

22. "Hood" makes a noun showing quality, state

Child	Childhood	Man	Manhood
Boy	Boyhood	Widow	Widowhood

23. "Ship" makes an abstract noun, showing quality

Friend	Friendship	Horseman	Horsemanship
Scholar	Scholarship	Lady	Ladyship
Author	Authorship	Citizen	Citizenship
Fellow	Fellowship	Student	Studentship

24. "Ance" makes an abstract noun

Attend	Attendance	Vigil	Vigilance
Allow	Allowance	Resist	Resistance
Assist	Assistance		

25. "Ist" makes noun, meaning "one who is"

Violin	Violinist	Race	Racist
Human	Humanist	Terror	Terrorist
Legal	Legalist	Guitar	Guitarist

Verb

26. "Trans" makes a verb with the sense "to carry"

Transport	to carry from one port to another.
Transatlantic	one which carries across the Atlantic Ocean.
Transform	which changes from one shape to another.
Transplant	to transport and sow a plant from one place to another.

27. "Port" makes a verb meaning "to carry"

Import	to carry into port
Deport	send a person away
Export	to carry out of port

29. "En" also changes a word into a verb

Haste	Hasten	Rough	Roughen
Quick	Quicken	Tough	Toughen
Broad	Broaden	Soft	Soften
Bright	Brighten	Hard	Harden
Light	Lighten		

30. "Ize" makes a verb, meaning "make"

Familiar	Familiarize	Terror	Terrorize
Liberal	Liberalize	Public	Publicize
Idol	Idolize	Flat	Flatness

31. "De" makes a negative verb

Claim	Declaim	Train	Detrain
Form	Deform	Plane	Deplane

Adverb

32. "Ly" turns an adjective into an adverb

Careful	Carefully	Haste	Hastily
Careless	Carelessly	Quick	Quickly
Slow	Slowly	Beautiful	Beautifully

Pronoun

33. "Ful" makes a positive pronoun

Care	Careful	Beauty	Beautiful
Duty	Dutiful	Hand	Handful

34. "Less" makes a negative pronoun

Care	Careless	Use	Useless
Worth	Worthless		

Negatives

35. "Il" makes a negative

Legal	Illegal	Literate	Illiterate
Legible	Illegible	Legitimate	Illegitimate

36. "Ir" makes a negative"

Regular	Irregular	Reversible	Irreversible
Recoverable	Irrecoverable	Resolute	Irresolute

37. "Dis" makes a negative, meaning "take away"

Arm	Disarm	Courage	Discourage
Belief	Disbelief	Loyal	Disloyal
Satisfaction	Dissatisfaction	Trust	Distrust

38. "Non" makes a negative, meaning "not"

Aggression	Non-aggression
Commissioned	Non-commissioned
Alignment	Non-alignment
Violence	Non-violence

39. "Anti" makes a negative

Climax	Anti-climax	Socialism	Anti-socialism
Body	Anti-body	Hero	Anti-hero

40. "Mis" means "wrong"

Adventure	Misadventure	Calculate	Miscalculate
Alliance	Misalliance	Carriage	Miscarriage
Behaviour	Misbehaviour		

41. "Mal" means "bad"

Practice	Malpractice	Treat	Maltreat
Education	Maleducation	Nourish	Malnourish

Prefixes

42. "Un" means "not"

Able	Unable	Ambitious	Unambitious
Known	Unknown	Touched	Untouched

44. "En" is a prefix that makes verbs

Courage	Encourage	Danger	Endanger
Roll	Enrol	Slave	Enslave
Able	Enable	Force	Enforce

45. "Poly" means "many"

Technical	Polytechnical	Flower	Polyflower
Clinic	Polyclinic		

46. "Pre" means "before"

Caution	Precaution	Occupied	Preoccupied
Eminent	Pre-eminent	Vent	Prevent

47. "Omni" means "all"

Present	Omnipresent	Potent	Omnipotent
Graph	Omnigraph		

48. "Super" means "above"

Man	Superman	Impose	Superimpose
Human	Superhuman	Natural	Supernatural
Abundant	Superabundant	Fine	Superfine

49. "Post" means "after"

Graduate	Post-graduate	Natal	Postnatal
Meridian	Postmeridian	Mortal	Postmortal
Operative	Post-operative		

50. "Micro" means "minute"

Photography	Microphotography
Phone	Microphone
Cosmography	Microcosmography (The description of man as a small world.)
Mania	Micromania (A delusion that one's body has become very small.)
Biology	Microbiology

51. "Hemi", "demi", "semi" mean "half"

Sphere	Hemisphere	Civilized	Semicivilized

Voice	Demivoice	Circle	Semicircle
Official	Demiofficial	God	Demigod

52. "Intra" means "within"

European	Intraeuropean	Group	Intragroup
Nuclear	Intranuclear	School	Intraschool
Continental	Intracontinental		
Departmental	Intradepartmental		

53. "Multi" means "many"

Purpose	Multipurpose	Graph	Multigraph
Lingual	Multilingual	Fold	Multifold
Millionaire	Multimillionaire		

54. "Macro" means "large"

Meter	Macrometer	Cosmic	Macrocosmic
Cosmology	Macrocosmology		
Mania	Macromania (a delusion that parts of the patient's body are bigger than they really are.)		

55. "Pseudo" means "false, untrue"

Socialist	Pseudosocialist	Classic	Pseudoclassic
Graph	Pseudograph	Mania	Pseudomania
Democrat	Pseudodemocrat		

56. "Ultra" means "beyond, exceeding"

Modern	Ultramodern	Micrometer	Ultramicrometer

Microscope	Ultramicroscope		

57. "Pan" means "all"

Islamic	Panislamic	Human	Panhuman
Harmonic	Panharmonic	American	Panamerican

58. "Neo" means "new"

American	Neoamerican	Genesis	Neogenesis
Mania	Neomania	Colonial	Neocolonial

Suffixes

59. "Dom" means "realm"

King	Kingdom	Free	Freedom
Prince	Princedom	Martyr	Martyrdom
Bore	Boredom	Fief	Fiefdom

60. "Ian" means "having a certain skill"

Logic	Logician	Statistic	Statistician
Beauty	Beautician	Magic	Magician

61. "Ism" means "system"

Social	Socialism	Hero	Heroism
Human	Humanism	Jingo	Jingoism
Capital	Capitalism	Commune	Communism
Communal	Communalism		

62. "Fy" or "ify" makes a verb meaning "to make"

Fort	fortify	Beauty	Beautify
Simple	Simplify	Test	Testify

63. "Ology" means "science of"

Climate	Climatology	Bacteria	Bacteriology
Zoo	Zoology	Crime	Criminology

64. "Able" means "which can be done"

Work	Workable	Touch	Touchable
Break	Breakable	Love	Loveable

65. "Er" means having quality

Drum	Drummer	Write	Writer
Sweep	Sweeper	Drive	Driver

CHAPTER IV

Words

The following words have been carefully selected to be of use to you in everyday application, whether writing or talking :

A

ABC : the rudiments of any subject.

Bernard Shaw said at the age of ninety, "I have yet to learn the ABC of politics."

Abhorrent : inspiring dislike.

Dishonesty is abhorrent to me.

Above-board : fair, open; undisguisedly.

He is an above-board gentleman.

Your work is above-board.

Abracadabra : spell, magic formula; gibberish.

There is no abracadabra to solve economic problems.

Political talk is all abracadabra.

Accommodating : obliging; easy to deal with; pliable, lax.

Good folk are always accommodating.

In social dealings you have to be accommodating.

Acumen : keen discernment; penetration.

Mrs. Indira Gandhi was a lady of acumen.

Adventitious : accidental: casual.

Your success in life is not adventitious.

Even good luck is not adventitious.

Affinity : relationship, love.

There is deep affinity between mother and son.

Agreeable : Pleasing; well-disposed, conformable.

Sea breeze is agreeable.

He is agreeable to your suggestion.

Truth is agreeable to all experience.

Allergic : sensitive to certain foods, medicines, etc.

Modern youth is allergic to good advice.

Anonymous : of unknown name; of unknown or undeclared authorship.

Many men who fought and died in the struggle of independence are anonymous.

Antagonism : active opposition.

There is a spirit of antagonism between snake and mongoose, fire and water, day and night, love and hate, life and death.

Appetizing : giving appetite; delicious.

Good food is appetizing.

Armageddon : End of the world, esp. in Jewish theology

Let us help stave off the thermonuclear Armageddon.

Articulate : express.

A newspaper articulates the aspirations of the people.

Asphyxiate : choke; suffocate.

Poverty asphyxiates a man as well as a nation. Dictatorship asphyxiates democracy.

Assimilate : digest; absorb into the system; harmonize.

Fruits and vegetables can be easily assimilated.

Minorities should be assimilated into the democracy.

B

Baccalaureate : B. A., university degree of bachelor.

Ram is baccalaureate in history.

Badger : bait like a badger, worry, tease.

"Boys, don't badger me, be off."

Ballyhoo : trumped-up publicity of a vulgar or misleading kind.

Ballyhoo can win battles but lose the war.

Bamboozle : hoax, mystify, cheat into doing something morally wrong or objectionable.

The dictators quite often bamboozle the people into war.

The thug befriended my son to bamboozle him out of money.

Bankruptcy : utter loss.

Modern men suffer from bankruptcy of discrimination which, as the Gita says, brought about the defeat and downfall of the Kauravs.

Banquet : sumptuous feast.

Modern civilization is a banquet of materialism.

Life is the flight of a bird through a floodlit banquet-hall, from darkness into darkness.

The king is at banquet, said Hamlet, not where he is eating, but being eaten by the worms.

Barrage : volley.

The Prime Minister faced a barrage of questions from the newsmen.

Today every nation has a barrage of problems.

Battalion **:** large body of men.

"Troubles come not as single spies but in battalions."

—*Shakespeare*

Beacon **:** signal-fire on pole or hill.

The beacon warned him of an approaching boat.

Truth should be the sole beacon of life.

Bedraggled **:** wet by trailing, hanging limp.

Babar had a bedraggled journey through the Khyber Pass for the conquest of India.

Beelzebub **:** the devil.

Beelzebub is up and playing havoc in modern civilization.

Bequeath **:** leave behind after death.

What more can you bequeath to posterity than honest work?

Bestride **:** get or sit with legs astride as on a horse or chair.

Confusion bestrides modern civilization.

A bold man bestrides his problems and difficulties.

Beyond **:** more than.

You have prospered beyond me.

Your talk is beyond understanding.

Bluster **:** storm boisterously.

You cannot win an argument by boasting and

blustering.

Brazen-Faced : shameless.

Ambition is a brazen-faced battle against competitors.

Browse : read for enjoyment.

Please browse through the book.

Buoyant : light-hearted; hopeful.

The Prime Minister's speech made the people buoyant about the future of the country.

C

Caesarism : autocracy.

Caesarism goes ill with democracy.

Cafeteria : restaurant in which customers fetch what they want from the counter.

Cafeterias are the hot bed of activity in colleges.

Cannibalize : to use one part of a similar machine to provide spare parts for others.

If you hand over your typewriter to this mechanic, it will be soon cannibalized.

Cantankerous : cross-grained, quarrelsome.

Keep a cantankerous fellow at an arm's length.

Caravanserai : an inn for travellers.

Caravanserai are very common in Turkey.

Castellated : castle-like; battlemented; having castles.

The *nouveau riche* (newly rich people) are fond of castellated mansions.

Catastrophe : disastrous end.

An air crash is a catastrophe.

Catechism : instruction by questions and answers.

Socrates, who never handled a pen, taught a lot through catechisms.

Chameleon : small lizard with power to change colours; inconstant person.

Chameleons do well in politics.

Chloroform : thin colourless liquid which when inhaled renders one insensible.

"Every man has his price," said Walpole, the Prime Minister of England, "and most men can be chloroformed with gifts, greed and graft."

Cinderella : person of unrecognised beauty of merit.

The film world is full of Cinderellas.

Commanding : impressive, exalted.

The Prime Minister has a commanding personality.

Cupidity : greed of gain.

Cupidity is a distinctive characteristic of the modern man.

Cushion : protect against shock or loss.

Money cushions a man against defeatism.

Crystallize : form into crystals of definite shape.

You should crystallize your views before you take action.

D

Dabble : engage in any pursuit, as a hobby.

It is dangerous to dabble in politics.

Daffodil : a pale-yellow-flowered narcissus; a delicate child.

The world today is not for daffodils.

Damocles : Greek who was feasted with sword hung by a hair over his head.

The sword of Damocles hangs over the head of every unemployed youth in the country.

Defector : one who leaves his party and joins another.

Indian politics full of defectors.

Demonetize : deprive money, currency, etc., of its status.

Hundred rupee notes need to be demonetized in India.

After a man retires, he is demonetized both at home and in the office.

Desperado : person ready for reckless criminal undertakings.

It is a job for the police to handle desperadoes.

Dexterity : skill, adroitness.

The police needs a good deal of dexterity to handle desperadoes.

Differentiate : discriminate: distinguish.

Few people today can differentiate vice from virtue.

Dilapidate : disrepair; decay.

Heavy rain dilapidated a building.

She lived in a dilapidated cottage.

Dilemma : argument forcing an opponent to choose one of two alternatives, both unfavourable to him.

A man without money and with domestic responsibilities is quite often on the horns of a dilemma. If he commits suicide, he dies, if he does not die, he does not know how to make ends meet.

Discommode : put to inconvenience.

A good man tries to discommode nobody except himself.

Disconsolate : unhappy; disappointed.

A greedy man; notwithstanding whatever you may do for him, is always disconsolate.

Doughty : valiant, rough, stout.

Doughty young men live happily and long.

Downtrodden : oppressed.

When you achieve economic heights, do not forget the downtrodden.

Dragoon : force into a course by persecution.

In democracy you cannot dragoon the people to do anything.

Dreamhole : hole left in wall of tower, etc. to admit light, music, etc.

Hope quite often is the only dreamhole in the God-forsaken prisonhouse of unemployment.

Dribble : flow; let flow, in drops or trickling stream.

When all is lost, hope still dribbles through.

Dryasdust : dull, laborious, uninteresting.

One has to drudge hard for a dryasdust competition.

Dubitation : doubt, hesitation.

With strong faith you can go ahead in any walk of life without dubitation.

E

Ebullient : boiling; exuberant.

He was ebullient with enthusiasm for victory.

You were ebullient in your oratory.

Don't be ebullient in praise of VIPs.

Egalitarian : holding the principle of equality in society.

It is best to be egalitarian in a democratic society.

Socialism means egalitarianism.

El Dorado **:** a mythical city abounding in gold.

Dempcracy has been El Dorado for the modern generation.

He failed to reach the El Dorado of a happy retirement.

Eloquence : The ability to speak or write well.

His speech was full of eloquence.

Emancipate : release.

Emancipation : freedom; salvation.

There is no emancipation without truth.

Truth alone can emancipate you.

Encyclopaedia : a book giving information on all branches of knowledge.

He is a walking encyclopaedia.

Your knowledge is encyclopaedic.

Enfant Terrible **:** child who asks awkward questions, repeats what he has heard, etc.

Feroze Gandhi was an *enfant terrible* in Indian Parliament.

No VIP wants an *enfantterrible in* a press conference.

Epicurean : one who believes that pleasure is the highest good.

Too many luxuries in the modern world have turned lot of people epicureans.

Equilibrium : state of balance, tranquillity.

Do not let wealth upset the equilibrium of your mind or head.

Eventuality : possible event.

Money is supposed to help in any eventuality; but quite often its lets you down where you least expect it .

Excreta : waste expelled from the body.

Material progress is excreta of the spirit.

Exhibitionism : tendency towards display or extravagant behaviour.

Indian marriages are plagued with exhibitionism.

Expeditiously : speedily.

You have to work expeditiously to meet deadlines.

Expertise : expert opinion, skill or knowledge.

In the modern world expertise fetches good price.

F

Facade : frontal or outward appearance.

Everything and everybody in the modern world is expected to have a fascinating facade.

Facetious : blunt; witty; shameless.

Nobody wants to keep company with a facetious fellow unless he is rich beyond the dreams of avarice.

Fait Accompli **:** a thing done and no longer worth arguing about.

Youth who inform their parents after their marriage treat it as a *fait accompli.*

Fantastic : extravagant, strange and wonderful.

A midnight safari is a fantastic experience.

Finical : over fastidious.

Do not be too finical about your clothes and food.

Flabbergast : dumbfound, astonish.

The father was flabbergasted to find his own son in competition against him.

Foolhardy : foolishly venturesome, delighting in needless risks.

It does not pay to be foolhardy and foppish to create a good impression on people.

Forlorn hope : desperate enterprise.

To get rich quickly is a forlorn hope.

Fritter : throw away time, money, energy on divided aims.

Prepare yourself for a big competition and do not fritter away your time on small trifles.

Fructiferous : bearing fruit.

Good deeds are greatly fructiferous.

G

Gallup Poll : test of how representative sample of public is to vote.

The Gallup poll showed that Jimmy Carter would win the Presidency of America against President Ford.

Gargantuan : enormous, gigantic.

All material achievements today are on the gargantuan scale.

Gastronome : judge of cuisine.

Today we have many gluttons but few gastronomes.

Genesis : origin.

What is the genesis of this quarrel in the house?

Generous : free in giving.

Don't be too generous with your love or with your contempt.

Gestapo : German secret state police of Nazi regime.

Nothing can be more dangerous to democracy than the Gestapo.

Gibberish : meaningless sounds.

Much of modern writing and public speaking is gibberish.

Gobbledegook : pompous official jargon.

Keep gobbledegook out of official communiques.

Goody-Goody : primly, pretentious, showily good; weakly virtuous.

More people try to be goody-goody than really capable of doing good.

Grandiloquent : pompous in language.

It does not pay to be grandiloquent in the company of intellectuals.

Gratuitous : got or given free.

Save yourself from a gratuitous insult.

Grotesque : comically distorted.

Modern painting is grotesque.

Grouse : grumble, complaint

Please let me know if you have any grouse against me.

Gumption : enterprising spirit.

Go, get rich quickly, if you have gumption for haste and waste, low thinking and high living.

Gusto : zest, special flavour.

Work with gusto for success.

H

Habeas corpus **:** writ requiring body of person to be brought before judge into court, especially to investigate lawfulness of his restraint.

No court in India can issue *habeas corpus* for a person arrested under Maintenance of Internal Security Act (MISA)

Habituate : to fall in the habit of.

A drunkard is habituated to liquor.

Halitosis : abnormally foul breath.

Unnatural food is the cause of halitosis.

Hallucinate : produce a false impression in the mind of.

Anybody can hallucinate with pelf, power and possessions.

Haphazard : mere chance.

Hazardous : risky, dangerous.

Too much truth can be hazardous.

Hercules : a hero of prodigious strength.

Poverty can break down even a Hercules.

Herculean : difficult as the tasks of Hercules.

To save the nation is always an Herculean task.

Heroi-comic : combining the heroic with the comic.

Most of the modern films based on the cult of violence are heroi-comic.

Hocus-pocus : jugglery, deception; typical conjuring formula.

Most of the modern achievements are hocuspocus.

Holus-bolus : all in a lump, altogether.

All his assets holus-bolus amounted to a petty sum.

Honoris causa : for the sake of honour; without remuneration.

Many societies have secretaries *honoris causa.*

Hotch-potch : hodge-podge, mixture of different things.

Everything in a social function is hotch-potch.

Hypertension : abnormally high blood pressure.

The price of political, social or commerical success is hypertension.

Hypochondria : morbid depression.

A suicide is the consequence of hypochondria.

Hysterical : morbidly emotional.

When you meet with a mishap, do not be hysterical.

I

Idiosyncracy : mental or physical peculiarity.

Every man has his idiosyncracies.

Ignoramus : ignorant person.

Go, learn what you don't know. Don't be an ignoramus.

Ignominy : dishonour, infamy.

Suffer ignominy rather than dishonesty.

Illuminate : throw light on.

This book illuminates the subject under discussion.

Imbroglio : confused heap.

After marriage the house is in imbroglio.

Immortalize : confer enduring fame on.

Plays have immortalized Shakespeare. Any good act, though unknown to anybody, immortalizes a man.

Impenetrate : penetrate deeply.

Water impenetrates any cotton cloth. Light impenetrates darkness.

You cannot impenetrate this subject.

Incertitude : uncertainty.

Let your commitments be without incertitude.

Indiscretion: imprudence.

An indiscretion can cost you your job.

Indistinguishable : without any difference.

Truth today is indistinguishable from propaganda.

Inferno : hell.

A skyscraper is a towering inferno.

Intelligentsia: intelligent educated people.

The intelligentsia keep out of political scrambles.

Intertwine : mix.

Joy is intertwined with sorrow.

J

Jaggery : coarse brown Indian sugar.

Jaggery is better for your health than white sugar.

Jardiniere : ornamental pot or stand for display of growing flowers in a room, on a window-sill, etc.

Jardiniere is a common feature of every modern sophisticated household.

Jekyll and Hyde: single person in whom two personalities alternate.

Every successful man is a Jekyll and Hyde in this competitive society.

Jeopardize: endanger.

Bluntness can jeopardize your chances of promotion, however truthful you may be.

Jettison : throw overboard.

When people rise to the top, they jettison many friends who helped them to rise.

K

Kaleidoscopic : having many-coloured variety.

You can get a kaleidoscopic view of the landscape from this window.

Kleptomania: irresistible tendency to steal in persons who are not otherwise needy.

Many affluent people suffer from kleptomania.

Knick-Knack : small dainty trifles.

Many kleptomaniacs pick up knick-knacks from shops.

L

Labyrinth : a complicated maze.

Life is a labyrinth which you should thread through with law and love, love of law, and law of love.

Lacerate : mangle, tear, afflict, distress.

The death of a child lacerates parents.

Lackadaisical : languishing, affected, sentimental.

Many a youth has a lackadaisical attitude.

Laissez Faire : free trade; freedom from government interference in trade and commerce.

Laissez-faire is now a dead economic doctrine, because trade is being politicized.

Languish : become feeble; lose vitality.

An industry languishes for want of demand.

Largesse : money or gifts from a patron.

Modern writers no longer live on largesse.

Lethargy : morbid drowsiness; great laziness.

Lethargy is thy greatest enemy.

Liaison : contact; relation.

He keeps liaison between his firm and the government.

Libido : emotional craving, leading to sexual activity.

Every individual and social action is not without a libido behind it.

Liquorish : greedy; longing.

One can be liquorish of money as well as moneyish of liquor.

Litterateur : literary man.

Litterateurs are usually impractical people.

Lixiviate : separate soluble and insoluble constituents.

Water can lixiviate sugar from sand.

Loquacious : talkative.

Loquacious people do well in society.

Lubricate : make slippery or smooth.

Graft lubricates official relations.

Luxuriant : abundant.

Hotels provide luxuriant surroundings for their guests.

M

Macabre : grim, gruesome.

The scene in the banquet hall after a drinking riot was simply macabre.

Machiavelli: unscrupulous schemer.

Only Machiavellis do well in diplomacy.

Emperor Aurangzeb's invitation to Shivaji was Machiavellian.

Magnetize : attract.

Money magnetizes men like bees.

Malafide : acting, done, in bad faith.

Nothing done in love is malafide.

Bad intentions make any action malafide.

Manipulate : to control something or some one to your advantage.

Accounts are manipulated to show losses instead of gains.

Maximize : increase to the utmost.

Industrial production has to be maximized to meet the needs of an increasing population.

Micawber : a sanguine idler trusting that some thing good will turn up.

Many a Micawber haunts the coffee houses, hoping to become ministers and millionaires.

Misdemeanour : offensive misbehaviour.

The clerk was expelled for misdemeanour.

Monotonous : dull; without variation.

Life in a factory is montonous.

Monumentalize : commemorate by building a monument.

Men monumentalize their achievements for historians.

Multifarious : having a great variety.

Science has invented multifarious gadgets for luxury.

N

Narcissism : tendency to self-worship.

There is much narcissism in lyrical poetry.

The nudes suffer from narcissistic tendencies.

Necessitate : force, compel.

Sickness necessitated his absence from office.

Neologism : coining of new words; new-coined word.

Every great and creative piece of writing is full of neologisms.

Ne plus ultra : impassable obstacle.

Speed greater than light is the *ne plus ultra* of journey to stars many light years away.

Nid-nod : keep nodding.

If you do not understand a speech, courtesy still demands that you nid-nod.

Nihilism : total rejection of current beliefs.

Most of the modern youth suffer from nihilism.

If you lose a job, do not be nihilistic.

Nincompoop : simpleton, person without sense or character.

The world today is full of knaves and nincompoops.

Nocturnal : of, in, done by, active in the night.

An owl is a nocturnal bird.

Notwithstanding : in spite of.

He failed in life notwithstanding his wealth and property.

Nucleus : central part.

The Prime Minister is the nucleus of the government.

Nugget : rough lump of native gold.

An honest youngster is a nugget.

O

Oasis : fertile spot in a desert.

Hope is an oasis in the desert of depression.

Obdurate : hardened; stubborn.

Modern youth are obdurate in their demands.

Objectivisim : tendency to lay stress on objectives.

There is a need for objectivism even in the study of a subjective matter.

Obliterate : blot out; efface, erase.

Time obliterates all sorrows.

Obnoxious : harmful; odious; offensive.

One has to put up with many obnoxious things in the world.

Ochlocracy : mob-rule.

Democracy has already given place to ochlocracy.

Officious : meddlesome.

The office workers should not be officious.

Ogygian : of obscure antiquity; prehistoric.

Archaeology is perpetually in search of ogygian objects.

Opprobrium : disgrace; infamy.

No opprobrium attaches to smuggling or black-marketing in high society.

Oscillate : swing.

Life oscillates between hope and despair.

Otherness : diversity; difference.

There is much otherness in death from life. But what is otherness in life from death?

P

Pageant : brilliant spectacle.

Life is a pageant to relish from a distance, but not one to get involved in.

Palliative : balm; medicine.

Courage is the best palliative in all difficulties of life.

Pandemonium : uproar; utter confusion.

Pandemonium prevailed in the conference hall.

Panorama : picture of landscape.

From a window in Simla you can see the whole panorama.

Panegyrize : speak, write, in praise of; eulogize.

Many journals in India do pretty little other than panegyrize the advertisers.

Papyraceous : of the nature of paper; as thin as paper.

They serve papyraceous wafers with tea.

Paramount : supreme.

Truth is paramount even in darkness like the sun is in the firmament.

Paraphernalia : miscellaneous belongings.

Modern tourism requires much paraphernalia for a comfortable journey.

Par excellence : the best example

A Prime Minister is *par excellence* the best politician in the country.

Pater-Familias : head of family.

Modern society does not recognise *pater-familias.*

Perambulate : walk, through, over or about.

You can perambulate in this garden.

Pertinacious : stubborn; persistent.

Youth should be flexible in response to life and not pertinacious in all dealings.

Philosophize : speculate; theorize.

To understand life you should philosophize on death.

Pinnacle : highest point.

The youth cannot wait for old age to achieve pinnacle of luxury and enjoyment.

Plethora : unhealthy increase.

Modern life is marked by a plethora of activities.

Post Mortem : after death.

Post mortem are increasingly used by the police to determine the cause of death.

Pow-wow : discussion.

I am going to have a pow-wow with my brother about his career.

Presumptuous : arrogant; unduly confident.

Do not be presumptuous about your success in I.F.S.

Putrescent : in process of rotting.

All old values have become putrescent today.

Q

Quadrennial : occurring every four years.

Presidential elections in USA are a quadrennial affair.

Quagmire : bog, mud, marsh.

The deeper you get into the quagmire of modern civilization, the more miserable you will be.

Quincentenary **:** 500th centenary.

The quincentenary of Guru Nanak's birthday was celebrated some years ago.

Quintessence **:** most essential part of something.

Joy is the quintessence of life.

R

Ragamuffin **:** ragged dirty fellow.

Ragamuffins may be hiding true gold of virtue.

Raison D'etre **:** purpose; reason; cause.

What is the *raison d'etre* of your being alive in the world? Concentrate on "Who am I" and one day you will know.

Rakish **:** smart and fast-looking.

Everything is rakish now-a-days.

Rampage **:** behaving violently.

Get away when a mob is on the rampage.

Rapprochement **:** recommencement of harmonious relations.

Simla Agreement has brought rapprochement between India and Pakistan.

Real-Politik **:** policy of placing one's own nation above all considerations.

Real-politik is predominant in international doctrine.

Recalcitrant : who does not agree on any terms.

Go smoothly with one who is recalcitrant to all reasonableness.

Retrogradation : backward motion.

What science calls progress is only retrogradation in real values of life.

Riff-Raff : common people

Democracy is the Government of the riff-raff.

Rigmarole : meaningless talk.

Ministers deliver rigmarole speeches.

Ruminate : ponder.

You should ruminate on the hows and whys of your life.

S

Sacrosanct : sacred; inviolable.

Everything is sacrosanct in democracy if done with the will of the people.

Salubrious : healthy (climate, food, air, etc.)

Sick people should live in the salubrious climate of the hills.

Salutiferous : promoting health.

Sweetmeats are not salutiferous to your health and happiness.

Sanctimonious : making a show of sanctity or piety.

Marriage should not be treated as a sanctimonious ceremony.

Sanguine : hopeful; bright; rosy.

I am sanguine about Rosie's success in the competition.

Saturnine : of gloomy temperament.

Old folk tend to become saturnine.

Savoir Faire : quickness to see and do the right thing, address, tact, etc.

Youth with savoir faire do well in society and professions.

Scandalize : offend moral feelings.

Do not scandalize people with foul language.

Sceptical : given to questioning truth of facts.

Modern youth are sceptical about all old values.

Schadenfreude : malicious enjoyment of others' misfortunes.

Those who are happy when you suffer, suffer from schadenfreude.

T

Tantamount : amounting to the same.

Your absence is tantamount to a French leave.

Teknonymy : the naming of parents from children.

The parents of successful children enjoy teknonymy.

Telaesthesia : an abnormal impression as of sense received from a distance.

With yoga, fasting and *tapasya* you acquire telaesthesia.

Televise : to transmit by television.

The Prime Minister's visit to Africa was televised.

Theanthropic : at once divine and human.

True saints and sages are theanthropic in their character and everyday life.

Theosophy : divine wisdom.

Madame H.P. Blavatsky founded the new school of theosophy as of ancient origin.

Thesaurus : a storehouse of knowledge.

A good dictionary is a kind of thesaurus.

Titillate : to stimulate : to tickle.

Flattery titillates everybody and only some theanthropic people can escape the stigma.

Topsy-Turvy : turned upside down.

The world becomes topsy-turvy for a person who is drunk with pelf, power and possessions.

Transubstantiate : to change to another substance.

Vice cannot be transubstantiated into virtue.

U

Ubiquitous : present everywhere.

Money is the ubiquitous medium of exchange.

Ultramundane : beyond the world.

Great yogis lead an ultramundane life.

Unison : complete agreement.

Politicians must work in unison with economists.

Uppish : pretentious; snobbish.

Those who try to be uppish finally meet their Waterloo sooner or later.

Utilitarian : looking to usefulness alone.

Many articles of daily use are utilitarian and few are artistic.

V

V-Sign : a sign made with the index and middle fingers in token of victory.

Prime Minister Winston Churchill won the second world war with his V-sign; and that is how the word originated.

Vacillate : (1) sway to and fro.

Life vacillates between hope and despair.

(2) Fluctuate in opinion or resolution.

He continued to vacillate between accepting or rejecting the offer.

Vainglorious : empty glory in one's performance.

Politicians win victories through vainglorious demonstrations.

Vanquish : to conquer; to overcome.

Truth cannot be vanquished by arms or charms.

Vehement : impetuous; forcible; urgent.

Babar delivered a vehement speech before the Battle of Panipat.

Vocabulary : list of words known to a person.

Shakespeare had a rich vocabulary.

You should enrich your vocabulary. Vocabulary is key to the storehouse of knowledge.

Vouchsafe : guarantee.

I vouchsafe the authenticity of this document.

W

Walkie-Talkie : a portable radio-telephonic transmitting and receiving set.

I don't want a walkie-talkie as my companion.

Warmonger : one who encourages war.

There is no war without war-mongers.

Wehrmacht : German armed forces specially between 1931-1945.

Hitler's Wehrmacht failed to win the world.

Will-o'-the-wisp : any elusive and deceptive person or thing.

Wordly success is a will-o'-the-wisp.

Worst : to defeat.

Churchill worsted Hitler in war.

X

Xenogenous : due to outside cause.

The birth of a wise girl like Ritu to a foolish mother can be considered xenogenous.

Xerophytic : able to withstand drought.

Thorny plants are usually xerophytic.

Y

Yoghurt : a semi-soild sourish food prepared from milk fermented by added bacteria.

I prefer curd to yoghurt.

Z

Zealous : full of zeal.

Falsehood is more zealous than truth.

Zephyr : a soft gentle breeze.

A zephyr blows on a summer morning.

Zigzag : road with turns and twists.

There is no zigzag road to truth.

CHAPTER V

Word Forms

Every word has a root which expands to different words because of grammatic conversions or customary usages.

When nouns are changed into verbs, pronouns, adverbs, adjectives, etc., the original form undergoes a minor operation, and sometimes even a major transformation, so much so that the original root stays buried and invisible underneath the surface.

You have got to learn these grammatic transformations to become proficient in the language. Some specimens are given below, but for fuller knowledge of many other words, you can go directly to the dictionary. In this case, as in many other cases, the regular use of a good dictionary is highly advisable.

ARISTOCRAT

Aristocrat : someone whose family has a high social rank.

Pandit Motilal Nehru was an aristocrat.

Aristocratic : one who belongs to the aristocracy, has characteristics which are considered to be typical of people of high social rank.

The Rockefellers are a highly aristocratic family.

Aristocracy : a class of people whose families have a high social rank and who hold special titles in some countries.

The Mughal Government was an aristocracy.

Aristocratically : in the manner of aristocrats.

Many of our politicians behave aristocratically rather than democratically.

COMMISSION

Commission : command; instruction; authority: body of persons having authority; percentage paid on amount involved, etc.

The Union Public Service Commission holds competitions for the top jobs in the Government of India.

Commissioner : an important official in a department.

Mr. Rajiv Walia is a Deputy Commissioner at Salem.

Commissionaire : uniformed door attendant at theatres, cinemas, large shops, etc.

Many M.A.'s are seeking jobs as commissionaires.

Commissariat : military department in charge of food

supplies.

Capt. Sinha was appointed as in-change of the commissariat.

Commissary : a shop that provides food equipment in a military camp or prison.

The Commissary at the prison was stocked weekly.

DOCTOR

Doctor : teacher; learned man; physician; holder of the highest university degree.

Doctorate : degree of doctor in a university.

I am working towards a doctorate in philosophy.

Doctoral : thesis written or done in order to obtain a doctor's degree.

A doctoral dissertation is not an easy task.

Doctrinaire : a person or attitude that insists on particular principles or theories without allowing argument against them.

Rammanohar Lohia was a doctrinaire of socialism.

FRUCTIFY

Fructify : to bear fruit; make fruitful; impregnate.

Good soil and water fructifies plants.

Fructiferous : bearing fruit.

Mango trees are fructiferous in summer.

Fructification : fructifying.

Without fructification a fruit tree is useless.

Fructuous : full of fruit; producing fruit.

This grape vine is very fructuous.

Fructose : a simple sugar found in honey and fruits.

Apples are rich in fructose.

MAGNET

Magnet : a piece of iron having the properties of attracting iron.

Magnets are useful in compasses because these point to the north when suspended.

Magnetic : having the properties of a magnet.

Jawaharlal Nehru had a magnetic personality.

Magnetically : like a magnet,

Mahatma Gandhi attracted the crowd magnetically.

Magnetism : power of attraction.

Her beauty had a definite magnetism.

Magnetize : to attract like a magnet; to give magnetic qualities.

Noble character magnetises a man.

PEDAGOGUE

Pedagogue : a teacher.

Dr. Radhakrishnan was a pedagogue before he

joined politics.

Pedagogical : of pedagogue.

Your speech at the college convention was rather pedagogical

Pedagogically : like a school teacher.

He behaved pedagogically, to the surprise of everybody.

Pedagogy : science of teaching.

Pedagogy has fallen on evil days.

POPULACE

Populace : the common people.

Democracy is a government of the populace.

Popular : enjoyed or liked by a large number of people.

Birth control has never been popular but it has to be enforced nevertheless.

Popularity : name and fame.

His popularity with radio audiences was immense.

Popularly : by the common people.

Mahatma Gandhi was popularly known as Bapu.

Popularize : to make popular.

Yoga, fasting and *tapasya* should be popularized.

Populate : inhabit a country.

While Russia and Australia are under-populated, India and China are overpopulated.

Population : total number of people.

The population of the earth has crossed the six billion mark.

REFORM

Reform: to become better, set of changes to improve a law or social system.

Religions need to be reformed.

Reformer : leader; one who makes people better.

Mahatma Gandhi was a great reformer.

Reformat : format anew.

He reformatted the disk.

Reformation : radical changes.

Guru Nanak brought about a great reformation in Indian society.

Reformative : tending or intended to produce reform.

Amendment to the Constitution of India is a reformative measure.

Reformist : ideas, activities, or people involved in trying to bring about reforms.

The government's adoption of reformist policies

was applauded.

SOPHIST

Sophist : ancient Greek teacher of philosophy and rhetoric, a captious or fallacious reasoner.

Many highbrow sophists haunt the coffee houses.

Sophism : false argument intended to deceive.

The cause of truth cannot be advanced through sophism.

Sophistic : deceptive.

Give up your sophistic arguments and let us seek truth.

Sophistically : in a high cultured way of modern society.

To rise in society you have to live sophistically.

Sophister : a student in some English universities.

Rosie is a sophister in Oxford.

Sophisticate : involve in sophistry; mislead; making artificial, make educated, cultured or refined.

Science is sophisticating the society.

Sophisticated : educated and refined, discriminating in taste and judgement, highly developed and complex.

Electronic machinery is highly sophisticated.

We are living in a sophisticated society.

Sophistry : Using clever arguments that sound convincing but are, in fact, false.

Intelligent people are seldom taken in by sophistry.

CHAPTER VI

Definitions

Some words have to be properly defined and explained to be properly understood for the purpose of systematic and scientific understanding.

Some such important words are given below.

Abecedarian

An Abecedarian poem is one consisting of all the letters of the alphabet, each line with an alphabetical letter in its proper order.

A-Bomb

An atom bomb is a missile causing devastation by setting off a chain reaction of molecular fission.

Acre

An acre is a piece of land measuring 4,840 square yards.

Acronym

An acronym is a name coined as acrostic, combining initials or initial syllables of the words in a long name or title.

Thus, USAID means United States Agency for International Development.

Acrostic

Set of lines in which initial letters spell out a message. Similar poem or series of prose lines in which final letters make a word or a message.

Action

Action in a drama or novel is the arrangement of incidents in the order of increasing interest. The action should progress steadily and fairly rapidly and lead directly to the point of culmination.

Air

Air is the gas forming the atmosphere of the earth, composed of approximately four-fifths nitrogen, and one-fifth oxygen with a small quantity of carbon dioxide, traces of rare gases and varying amounts of water vapour.

Alibi

The plea of having been, at the alleged time of the commission of an offence, elsewhere than the alleged place of commission.

Americanism

An Americanism is a word or phrase used in America, that differs in form or meaning from the expression that would commonly be used in Britain to mean the same thing.

Anachronism

An anachronism is something or someone that seems very out of date or old-fashioned or something in a book, play, film that seems wrong because it could not have existed at the historical period depicted.

Anglicized word

An anglicized word is one which came from a foreign language and is now modified in some way such as in pronunciation to conform to native English word habits.

Argot

Secret language of thieves and vagabonds.

Articulation

Expression of orderly thought in appropriate phrasing.

Bacteriophage

Destroyer of disease germs, antibiotics which destroy bacteria.

Bibliography

List of books and articles given to indicate sources consulted in the preparation of a composition, and to help persons interested in the same subject to find material on it.

Biopsy

Removal and examination of living tissue for diagnosis.

Biotic

Related to life or living things.

Blockbuster

1. An aerial bomb weighing more than four tons.
2. A smash hit, movie, novel or drama.

Blue Angel

A barbiturate sleeping pill.

Brainwashing

Forcing someone to believe something by continually telling them or showing them evidence that it is true and preventing them from considering other evidence.

Carpet-Bagger

A politician not resident in a district but residing there purely for political advantages.

Censorship

Imposition of arbitrary standards on what can be read, written, spoken, heard, drawn or acted.

Chaperone

A married woman who accompanies or watches over unmarried women for the sake of propriety.

Classical

Excellent in conformity with established principles and traditional cultural criteria.

Climax

The culminating point of a series of ideas, words, sentences, situations presented in the order of increasing importance.

Commuter

Traveller who changes and reduces the cost of his transportation by paying fares in advance.

Daylight Saving Time

Setting back the clocks to make summer days seem longer.

Deep Freeze

Refrigeration at a much lower temperature than that of an ice box.

Deep Freeze Locker

Refrigerator for storage of food and other organic substances at temperatures below 32 degrees F.

Denouement

The explanation of something that has previously been unclear or that has been kept secret, especially at the end of a book or play.

Diacritical

A mark over or on a letter to distinguish its sound from others represented by the same letter.

Determinist

Philosopher who believes that outside causes limit or control economic and social progress and acts of the individual will.

Electronarcosis

Treatment of mental disorders by feeding into the brain a relatively weak electrical current, an improvement of shock therapy.

Etymological Fallacy

The erroneous belief that the meaning of a word at some earlier period (especially in its earliest known form) or in some cognate language is decisive in determining the current meaning of the word.

Euthanasia

Painless death or assisted suicide, now generally held to mean the practice of putting incurable invalids painlessly to death.

Gallicism

A French expression translated word for word rather than made to conform to the English medium.

Genetics

The science of the origin of individuals through heredity.

Historical Present

The use of present tense to describe past events vividly.

Histrionics

Theatrical oratory.

Incommunicado

Without privilege or possibility of communication.

Jitterbug

1. a nervous person
   Anil is a total jitterbug.
2. a fast popular dance
   Do you know how to dance the jitterbug.
3. a person fond of dancing this
   Smita is a jitterbug while Anita loves the tango

Journalese

A cheap and gaudy style as found in yellow sensationalist journalism.

Kangaroo Court

An improperly constituted or illegal court.

I refuse to allow this kangaroo court to procede.

Liaison

1. Illicit cohabitation.

He carried on the dangerous liaison with her, despite being warned.

2. Communication or Cooperation, especially between military forces or units.

Capt. Roy was appointed as liaison between the forces.

Malapropism

Wrong word chosen because of confusion between words of similar sound or appearance but of utterly different meaning. Thus, calling angels as "angles" will be a malapropism.

I believe in naturalism not socialism.

Nebula

Cloudlike concentration of billions of stars remote from our system.

Obscurantism

Opposition to enlightenment and progress.

Onomatopoeia

A word in which sound imitates the sense as

"gurgling" which indeed sounds like gurgling.

Palindrome

A word or a group of words that is the same when read backward or forward, e.g., "Malayalam".

Spoonerism

An unintentional ludicrous distortion of words through transposing initial letters.

Students *hissed* their *mystery* class today.

Unbeknownst

Without having been known.

The king helped the poorest unbeknownst.

CHAPTER VII

One-Word Substitutes

There are words which embody the meaning of several words. These words are very useful for abbreviations, paraphrasing, telegraphy, and general literary dynamism.

It is essential that you should learn these words to add salt and spice to your style and literary perfection.

Some of these words are given below by way of samples:

A

Archipelago : a group of islands.

Aristocracy : a government by the upper classes; a ruling body of nobles.

Augmentative : having the property of increasing.

Auscultation : listening to the movement of theheart.

Auspicious : of good omen.

Automatic : working of itself.

Avalanche : mass of snow, earth and ice descending swiftly from mountain.

Avatar : descent of deity to earth in an incarnate form.

B

Behaviourism : doctrine that gives adequate knowledge, all human actions admit analysis into stimulus and response, and that ability to predict them depends on exhaustive study of behaviour in that light.

***Bona fide* :** done in good faith.

Botanical : relating to the scientific study of plants.

Breakdown : analysis of cost, etc. into its component parts.

Burglar : one who breaks into a house at night with the intent to commit felony.

Burlesque : imitation for purpose of deriding or amusing.

C

Centrifugal : tending to fly away from centre.

Centripetal : tending to fly towards the centre.

Ceremonious : showing addiction to ceremony.

Certificate : a document formally affirming a fact.

Certiorari : writ from higher court for records or cases tried in lower courts.

Co-education : education of boys and girls together.

D

Dazzle : confuse or dim sight of a person with excess of light.

Distraught : violently agitated.

Dramatize : to present as a play.

E

Evaporate : turn from solid or liquid into vapour.

Evolution : appearance of events in proper succession.

Excavate : make hollow by digging.

Exchequer : department of public service charged with receipt and custody of revenue.

Experience : actual observation or practical acquaintance with facts and events.

Expressionism : modern tendency among painters, dramatic authors, architects, etc., to subordinate realism to the symbolic or stylistic expression of the artist's or character's inner experience.

G

Galatea : superior striped cotton dress material.

Guarantee : thing given as security for fulfilment of certain conditions or permanence.

H

Heuristic method : system of education under which the pupil is trained to find out things for himself.

Hibernate : spend the winter in a state of deep sleep like animals buried in or under snow.

Hierarchy : any graded organization.

I

Inexhaustible : that which cannot be finished.

Inexplicable : which cannot be explained.

Infatuate : inspire with extravagant passion.

Inexpressible : that cannot be expressed in words.

Infidel : disbeliever in true religion.

Infighting : fighting within a group.

Isotope : one or two or more forms of an element differing from each other in weight of atoms.

J

Jabber : speak volubly and with little sense.

Jactitation : offence of falsely claiming to be a person's wife or husband.

Jaggery : coarse brown Indian sugar made from palm sap.

K

Kibitka : a circular tent covered with felt.

Kimono : long loose Japanese robe with wide short sleeves held together by a sash.

Kibbutz : a farm, factory or workplace in Israel where the workers live together and share all the duties and income.

L

Laminate : 1. several thin layers of material such as wood or plastic stick together. 2. Cover a product with a thin sheet of clear plastic in order to protect it.

Lineament : distinctive features or characteristics especially of face.

Linotype : a trademark for a printing machine that is operated by a keyboard like a typewriter and that holds each time it types on one piece of metal.

Liquefy : bring solid or gas into liquid form.

Lodgement : a place where something can stick or remain firmly.

M

Macaroon : a sweet biscuit flavoured with almonds or coconut.

Matador : man appointed to kill bull in a bullfight.

Minerva : Roman goddess of wisdom.

Miniature : 1. something which is very small, especially a very small version of something which is normally much bigger. 2. A very small painting, especially of a person.

Minion : a person who has a very unimportant job, especially one who carries out someone else's orders.

N

Non-resident : not residing in the place in question.

Nostalgia : a slightly sad and very affectionate feeling you have for the past especially for a very happy time.

Nostrum : 1. a kind of medicine prepared and sold by someone not fully qualified. 2. someone's favourite idea or theory, which is intended to solve a particular problem.

O

Obliterate : to remove completely.

Obsequious : people who are too eager to help you, listen to what you say, agree with you, etc.

Obscurantism : the practice of deliberately making something vague and difficult to understand, especially to prevent people from finding the truth.

P

Pamphlet : a very thin book with only a few pages and a paper cover produced to tell people about a particular subject.

Patricide : the murder of one's own father.

Patrimony : inheritance from father or ancestors.

Philology : the study of words, especially the woods in a particular language, and how they have developed or changed.

Q

Quagmire : 1. a soft, wet area of land that you sink into if you try to walk on it. 2. an awkward, complicated, or embarrassing situation.

Quadrillion : a million raised to the fifth power.

Qualm : a qualm is a feeling of doubt or nervousness

that you have because you are not sure that what you are doing is right.

R

Rabelaisian : marked by exuberant imagination.

Rejuvenate : to make young again.

Rationalism : a system of belief regulated by reason, not authority.

Recapitulate : to go over the chief points again. Redemption: the process of being redeemed.

S

Sanctuary : 1. a place of safety for someone 2. a place where birds or animals are protected.

Siphon : 1. draw a liquid out of a container through a tube using atmosphere pressure.

2. a tube used for siphoning.

Siren : a sea-nymph, part woman, part bird, whose songs lured sailors to death.

Spasm : a violent involuntary muscular contraction.

Spontaneous : not planned or arranged, people who behave in this fashion.

Squeamish : easily shocked or upset by unpleasant sights or situations.

Stanchion : a post or pillar, an upright support, a vertical strut.

Staccato : a noise consisting of a series of short separate sounds.

T

Tabernacle : a small text which contained the most sacred writings of the ancient jews and which they took with them when they travelled.

Tantamount : amounting to as much or to the same.

Terrestrial : of or existing on the earth; living or growing on land or on the ground rather than in the sea.

Topography : study and description of the physical features of land.

Trebuchet : a medieval military engine for launching stones.

Trinomial : consisting of three words.

Trilingual : using three languages.

Triumphant: victorious or successful 2. exultant.

U

Ultrasonics : the science and application of ultrasonic waves

Undertaker : one who takes in hand an enterprise;

one who buries the dead.

Unmistakable : that which cannot be mistaken or doubted.

V

Vacillate : 1. fluctuate in opinion or resolution.

2. move from side to side.

Verification : establishing the truth or validity of something.

Vogue : 1. the prevailing fashion 2. popular use or currency.

W

Wallow : 1. to roll about in mud. 2. indulge in unrestrained pleasure or misery.

Wampum : beads made from shells used as money.

Welter weight : a weight in certain sports between lightweight and middleweight.

X

Xylophone : a musical instrument of wooden or metal bars graduated in length.

Y

Yarborough : a Bridge hand containing no card above a nine.

Z

Zoology : the scientific study of animals, especially with reference to their structure, physiology, classification, and distribution.

CHAPTER VIII

Ideas Make Words

Ideas make words. Great ideas find great words. If you have a strong idea to embody and express, you will always manage to find suitable words to clothe your ideas.

Look at new-born babies and pet animals! They do not know a single word of human vocabulary. Yet by means of sounds and gestures they manage to convey their ideas to others, the spectators, and particularly the people who are in love with them, or a nurse who looks after a child.

Words, after all, are born of sounds. Human sounds have been concentrated and codified in the form of words. Every syllable represents a sound; and every word is a blend of different sounds. If a baby or a pet animal goes on making sounds to express his meaning, he does finally succeed in doing that.

But consider a grownup person who is not at all

innocent of human vocabulary like a babe or a pet animal! He has an understanding of some human language right from his childhood. If he properly uses the words he does know, he can employ them to express any idea he pleases, however great or complicated it may be.

Greatest Ideas in the Simplest Words

The greatest ideas of the world can be clothed in the simplest of words.

Look at the Bible! How simple is its language and yet how sublime. There is no greater writing than the *Sermon on the Mount;* and yet Jesus Christ has couched his message in the simplest words that common, unlettered men and women would understand.

This increase *Sermon on the Mount,* intended for simple, uneducated folks is so sublime that it has held the greatest scholars spellbound for two thousand years.

So it is not bombastic words that can do the trick and win laurels for you. The simplest words properly arranged can perform a magic which is beyond the power and capability of the greatest intellectuals.

The More Words You Use, The More Words You Learn

The right way to increase your word power is not to enrich your vocabulary before putting your pen to paper and start using them for essays, letters, and everyday purposes of life. That way you will merely confuse yourself and may never learn the right use of words you have treasured in your memory.

Learn the right use of the few words you already know; and as you go on learning more words, pigeonhole them properly in your memory by using them in everyday communication. You are likely to conquer a new kingdom in the world of vocabulary which must be consolidated as well as expanded. You must consolidate the territory you have already conquered before you make new acquisitions and annexations.

Learn From Shakespeare

Shakespeare had a rich vocabulary; but he did not learn all those words before he started writing plays. Shakespeare's vocabulary in the early plays is not so rich as in his later plays, which shows that he expanded his vocabulary as he achieved maturity, but he consolidated his kingdom of words as he went on conquering more words.

While we are wonderstruck by the luxuriance of Shakespeare's vocabulary, we are also awestruck by his manipulation of the simplest words to express the greatest ideas. Just imagine what power has been concentrated in these words:

To be or not to be, that is the question

All the jargon of the astute scholars is unable to clothe the sweetness, strength and sublimity of the idea contained therein. It is because with Shakespeare, ideas came first and the words afterwards. He found words to clothe his ideas, not ideas to accommodate in the shell of his words, as many of the modern scholars do.

Keep a Notebook

Great ideas are not manufactured in the intellectual laboratory of the great scholars, intellectuals and philosophers. Great ideas are born out of inspiration. These flashes of inspiration do not come all the time or when and where you want them to come. Great ideas flash across your mind at the most unexpected moments. Therefore, you should note them as they come.

When you have noted and collected, systematize and arrange your stray ideas, flitting like birds through the floodlit banquet-hall of your mind, you will find that these combine to make the best of your writings.

Keep a Diary

Keep a small diary and jot down the great ideas as these flash across the screen of your mind. You should put them in black and white as these appear on the stage of your consciousness. If you are walking on the road, halt a moment to jot down a great idea passing through you mind. By the time your reach your destination, it will have passed out altogether and be forgotten.

Great ideas are like your guests. You must welcome them and entertain them while they are passing through your head. They are jet-age tourists in a hurry. If you do not meet them when you can, you lose them forever.

Sample of a Diary

Note below the ideas, which were taken down as they came and note how they express great thoughts in the simplest words.

January 16

Why do you expect God to treat you differently from the way you maltreat a grain of wheat—floored and floured, kneaded when needed, pushed and crushed, beaten and eaten, jawed and mawed ?

January 17

I am terribly fed up with all that I am feeding on, and yet I cannot check myself from the yawning pit of bottomless guilt.

January 21

Honesty is impossible in a society in which everybody wants the maximum for his work. It is possible where people are taught to expect little or nothing, and do not care for name, money or fame but treat life as a duty to be done.

January 23

If you marry, children may come with more responsibilities, and they generate troubles from generation to generation. It is better to stop a chain of troubles at the source.

January 27

Sleeping in a warm bed in winter is like eating chilled food in summer. You are likely to get lost in the luxury and may never swim to the top.

January 28

Men with money have a lot of self-assurance but they stand on stilts. Once the stilts are removed, they collapse. True self-assurance is born when you own nothing.

January 29

SEX—When l/10th of the steam comes out of a tiny aperture, it drives the locomotive, but when 9/10th escapes at once, it merely blows a whistle.

January 30

This day of Gandhiji's assassination must be regarded as the most important day in the politics of India. On that night every year the Right Thinkers should keep a night-long vigil on the samadhi of Gandhiji—a silent, deep session—to let great ideas from the unknown seep through the mind. No other day, except Guru Teg Bahadur's Martyrdom Day is worth celebrating.

January 31

If a man is honest, accounting of money is unnecessary; and if he is dishonest, accounting of money is useless because he can always cook accounts.

February 2

Trifles can torture the mind. So remove the thorns while you can, lest one day you have to sleep on a bed of thorns.

February 4

If you don't control death while you live, you control life while you die.

February 5

Emergency is the noncomitant of technological civilization. While we hug this false civilisation, we are bound to have emergencies in the individual, in the home, in the society, office, business, country and the world.

February 9

God is the greatest prankster who laughs at the contrivances to enforce his inviolable laws which few can understand and many merrily misunderstand.

To lie to a liar is truth because two negatives make a positive.

February 11

Sufferings are not the punishment but the rewards of righteous life.

February 14

Ninety per cent of the people in the world are negative; but a good negative makes a good positive.

February 16

We seek ease and therefore we get disease.

February 18

I don't need money. I don't think money. I don't want to work for money. If a work is not worth doing without money, it is not worth doing at all.

February 19

Anything spiritual is best; supernatural is better; natural is good; unnatural is bad; anti-natural is worse; artificial is worst.

February 21

To toe the line of competition is beastly. One should keep exerting himself without rewards.

February 24

Don't be tempted by a taste that leaves behind a distaste.

February 25

So long as you are bound with money, you are bound to go wrong. So long as you do not rise above pelf, power and possession, you cannot think good, do good or be good.

February 26

There is no difference between the house and the jungle. There is a house in the jungle. Here is a jungle in the house.

February 29

The only holiday I know is the holiday from troubles. That holiday comes from right thoughts, right words and right deeds.

CHAPTER IX

Idioms

Prepositions are a very important part of sentence construction.

Prepositions have to be carefully understood, because with the change of the preposition you change the meaning of the sentence.

These prepositional usages, known as idioms, are very important for enriching your vocabulary. Knowing an idiom, without its proper usage is quite useless, like pearls cast before the swine.

The following few words and their prepositional idioms are given by way of an example. You have to learn more and more of them, as you come across them in books and newspapers, writings and speeches, dialogues and discourses.

ACT

To act on : to exert an influence on : to act in accordance with.

Acid acts on iron.

You should act on your father's advice.

To act up to : to fulfil; to come in practice up to the standard of.

He acted up to high principles and achieved great success in life.

BRING

To bring up : to rear.

The boy was brought up by his uncle.

To bring about : to cause to happen : to bring to pass, effect; to turn round.

Mrs. Indira Gandhi brought about great changes in the country.

To bring down : to humble; to shoot; to overthrow; to lower.

The hunter brought down a pigeon.

Do not bring down the honour of your nation.

To bring down the house : to call forth a general applause.

Prime Minister's speech brought down the house.

To bring forth : to give birth; to produce.

Trees bring forth flowers and fruits.

To bring forward : to advance in book-keeping.

Rs. 10,045 were brought forward on the day book.

To bring home : to impress; to prove.

Importance of 20-Point Programme has been brought home to the people.

To bring in : to introduce; to yield; to pronounce a verdict.

The farm brought in a rich harvest.

To bring off : to rescue, to achieve.

They brought off the drowning sailors.

To bring on : to induce; to cause to advance.

They brought on the forces for a final showdown.

To bring out : to make clear or prominent : to put before the public, such as book, play, etc., to introduce in society.

Hind Pocket Books have brought out many works of fiction.

To bring over : to convert.

After the Emergency, the Congress has brought over many opponents.

To bring to : to restore to consciousness.

The doctor lost the hope of bringing to consciousness

the unconscious patient.

To bring under : subdue.

Akbar could not bring under Maharana Pratap.

To bring up : to rear; educate; to introduce to notice; to make prominent; to vomit.

Children should be brought up as simply as possible

—Queen Victoria.

To bring up the rear : to come last.

CARRY

To carry all before one : to bear down all opposition.

Prime Minister Indira Gandhi is carrying all before her.

Carry away : to carry off; to be excited; to transport.

If one person misbehaves, all should not be carried away.

Carry it : to brave; demean oneself; to gain the advantage; carry the day.

If you have won a hard battle, you are entitled to carry it.

To carry off : to cause the death of; to gain; to win as a trophy; to come to pass muster.

Coronary thrombosis carries off millions every year.

To carry on : to manage; continue; proceed; complain or behave unrestrainedly.

Who is now carrying on your father's business after his death?

To carry one's point : to overrule objection to one's plan or view.

The party in power manages to carry its point.

To carry out : to accomplish.

Have you carried out the order of your boss?

To carry over : to bring into the other party, to take to the next page, as an account; to postpone to next occasion.

The Bill was carried over to the next session of Parliament.

To carry the day : to be successful; to win a victory.

Babar carried the day in the First Battle of Panipat.

To carry through : to perform; to support through difficulties; to succeed in putting into effect.

The minister carried through the day's engagements.

To carry too far : to continue beyond reasonable limits.

Students should not carry agitations too far.

To carry up : to continue to build upward; to trace back.

A skyscraper has to be carried up.

To carry weight : to possess authority; to have force.

Your opinion does not carry weight in Parliament.

DIE

To die away : to disappear by degree, become gradually inaudible.

Old customs are dying away.

To die down : to subside; to die above ground, leaving only roots underneath.

The rose bush has died down.

Opposition to Emergency has died down.

To die game : to keep up one's spirit to the last.

The great soldiers prefer to die game.

To die hard : to struggle hard against death; to be long in dying.

Old habits die hard.

To die off : to die quickly or in large numbers.

Millions died off in the recent China earthquake.

To die out : to become extinct.

Dodos have died out.

EAT

To eat away : to destroy gradually.

Water eats away iron.

To eat in : the action of acid.

Acid eats in metals.

To eat off : to clear by setting the cattle to eat.

This meadow can be eaten off.

To eat out : to finish eatables; to encroach upon.

His property was eaten out by squatters.

To eat up : to devour entirely.

All his savings were eaten up by his niece and nephews.

FALL

Fall among : to find oneself in the midst of.

He fell among the thieves.

To fall away : to decline gradually; to languish; to grow lean; to revolt.

Many Ananda Margis have fallen away.

To fall back : to retreat, give way.

When Hitler attacked, Russians fell back temporarily.

To fall back upon : to have recourse to.

In times of need you can always fall back on good friends.

To fall behind : to lag; to be in arrears.

Your account is falling behind for the last two months.

To fall for : to become enamoured of.

He fell for a beautiful girl.

To fall in with : to agree; to comply with; to meet by chance.

He fell in with a group of no gooders.

To fall off : to become detached and drop.

The lid fell off the jar.

To fall on : to begin eagerly; to attack; to meet.

They fell on the enemy at night.

To fall out : to quarrel.

The dacoits fell out over the distribution of the loot.

To fall short : to be insufficient.

Sugar fell short for the banquet.

To fall through : to fail; to come to nothing.

All my ambitions have fallen through.

To fall upon : to begin hastily and eagerly.

The children fall upon comics.

GET

To get along : to make progress ; advance.

How is your child getting along at school ?

To get away with : to carry a thing through.

Many politicians get away with illegal activities.

To get off : to escape.

It is not easy to get off from jail.

To get out : to extricate; to produce; to take oneself to.

How are you going to get out of this trouble?

To get over : to surmount; to recover.

You can get over malaria with quinine.

To get round : to circumvent; to persuade.

Get round your parents with your friends help.

To get through : to finish; to telephone.

Have you got through to your father?

CHAPTER X

Idiomatic Phrases

Many idiomatic phrases are now outdated and you need not burden your memory with memorizing them. Nergis Dalal had written an interesting article on the subject in *Times of India:*

> Some years ago when I was correcting English examination papers for pre-university students, one of the questions that created the most problems in understanding was one where the students had to explain some of the curious colloquial phrases that have crept into the English language. There was always one such question, and for children whose native language was not English, it proved infinitely baffling. And who can blame them?
>
> Take the much-used phrase *no room to swing a cat* meaning very cramped quarters. The students had never heard of such a thing, but one

of them intelligently worked it out this way. He had heard that the English as a race were very fond of animals, so perhaps one eccentric individual was fond of erecting a swing for his cats, in which they could play, and any room which was too small was one in which his pampered cats could not ride up and down. I gave him full marks, although the origin of this phrase is very different, dating back to the times when the British had unthinking cruel customs involving animals. The custom was to hang up a leather sack in which a live cat was put, to make a swinging target for archery. *No room to swing a cat* therefore meant not enough space for archery practice.

Another phrase which turned up regularly was *to show the white feather.* This was interpreted variously and often in many ingenious ways, but no one felt that it could mean to act the coward. This phrase originated with cock-fighting, when a bird which had even one single white feather in its tail, was thought always to run out of the ring when attacked.

I am not sure if this question is still being included in English language papers, but the world's most renowned linguists would certainly disapprove. There is an increasingly strong feeling that what is considered bad sor incorrect English is often simply a matter of English vocabulary superimposed on the grammar and philological system of the native speaker and that English as a second language should be taught for purposes of efficient communication and understanding.

Indian English is full of phrases which are now so common that no one raises an eyebrow. *I like to take coffee* (a confession of theft?) and *everyone blames the youth for today's ills* are quite usual !

Is it really necessary for the English student to know what *trailing a red herring* means or why anyone should be *as right as a trivet? To buy a pig in a poke, once in a blue moon,* is not because one is not *yet dry behind the ears,* but simply because one had fallen, *hook, line and sinker* for what one imagined was the real *McCoy !*

A

Account : *To go to one's long account* : to die.

Customs of yesteryears have gone to long account.

Sooner or later, all of us will go to long account.

Add : *To add fuel to the fire:* to increase the trouble.

When there is a quarrel in the family, a few neighbours enjoy adding fuel to the fire.

Air : *To give oneself airs* : to feel proud.

When you have passed an examination and secured a great victory, do not give yourself airs, because behind one examination there is another examination like a mountain behind a mountain.

All : *All in all :* complete master.

I am all in all in the house today.

For good and all : finally.

He left the house for good and all.

Answer : *To answer the call of nature :* to ease oneself; to defecate.

The villagers who have no lavatories in their houses go out into the fields to answer the call of nature.

Apostle : *An apostle of doom :* pessimist; who predicts trouble and bad days ahead.

Baghi is an apostle of doom and warns everybody against coming evils which may not come.

April : *April fool :* one sent on a use errand on April 1st.

It is permissible to make an April fool of someone, whether friend or foe.

Arms : *To lay down one's arms* **:** to surrender.

It is better to lay down one's arms than to die unnecessarily.

B

Back : *To go back on one's word :* to break one's promise.

Great souls never go back on their word, whatever the consequence unless it is absolutely necessary to conform to the spirit and not the letter of a promise.

Bad : *To be in one's bad books :* to be in disfavour.

If you hesitate to flatter your boss, you will find yourself in his bad books.

Bag : *To leave bag and baggage :* to clear out completely.

It took a lot of litigation on the part of the landlord before his tenant left bag and baggage.

To let the cat out of the bag : to disclose a secret.

If you bribe the servant, he will let the cat out of the bag.

Ball : *To keep the ball rolling :* to keep things going.

It is the duty of the head of the family to keep the ball rolling.

The ball at one's feet : success in one's grasp.

If you don't prepare for I.F.S. do not expect the ball at your feet.

Bark : *To bark up the wrong tree :* to follow the wrong clues.

In following criminals, detectives cannot afford to bark up the wrong tree.

His bark is worse than his bite : his angry words are worse than his punishment.

He is short-tempered but his bark is worse than his bite.

Bay : *Keep at bay* : to keep away.

Keep all domestic troubles at bay.

To stand at bay : to face an enemy at close quarters.

When the Mughals attacked the Sikhs, the latter stood at bay.

Beat : *To beat about the bush* : to approach a subject in an indirect manner.

Please do not beat about the bush and let me know at once what I can do for you.

Blanket : *Wet blanket* : a damper of spirits; a killjoy.

A death in the family at the time of a marriage is a wet blanket.

On the wrong side of the blanket : illegitimately.

The child was born on the wrong side of the blanket.

Bud : *To nip in the bud* : to destroy at its very beginning.

Evil should be nipped in the bud.

C

Catch : *To catch a Tartar* : to attack a stronger foe than oneself.

In the technological march, the man had caught a Tartar.

Certain : *In a certain condition :* pregnant.

The doctor found the girl in a certain condition.

Chalk : *By a long chalk :* by a considerable distance/difference.

They won the cricket match by a long chalk.

Not to know chalk from cheese : to know nothing about the matter.

In textiles and fabrics, I do not know chalk from cheese.

Chance : *An eye to the main chance :* thought for self-enrichment.

Everybody enters trade with an eye to the main chance.

Cloth : *To cut one's coat according to one's cloth :* to live within one's means.

If you do not cut your coat according to your cloth, you will find yourself in trouble.

Coal : *To carry coal to Newcastle :* to engage in a futile profession or pointless activity.

Selling ice to the Eskimos is like carrying coal to Newcastle.

To heap coal of fire on the head : to excite remorse by returning good for evil.

Mahatma Gandhi heaped coal of fire on the head of the Pathan who was sent to kill him.

D

Dagger : *At daggers drawn :* in a state of hostility.

Moscow and Peking cannot forever be at daggers drawn.

Look daggers : to look in a hostile manner.

The woman looked daggers at the step-child.

Dance : *To dance to one's tune :* to be slavish.

If you do not dance to your boss's tunes, you will be fired.

Dance upon nothing : to be hanged.

For your anti-national activities one day you will dance upon nothing.

To lead one a dance : to keep one involved in a series of wearisome activities.

The girl led her father a dance.

Die : *The die is cast :* an irrevocable step has been taken; there is no turning back.

The board took the decision to fail him, the die is cast.

Down : *Down in the mouth :* in low spirits.

In the non-violent, non-cooperation movement,

India was never down in the mouth.

E

Edge : *To edge in a word :* to get a word in with difficulty.

When the minister was talking, his PA tried to edge in a word.

To play with edge tools : to deal carelessly with dangerous matters.

In politics do not play with edge tools.

Eye : *To hit the bull's eye :* to reach the target.

To get a good job you should hit the bull's eye.

F

Face : *To fly in the face of :* To set one self directly against.

You should not fly in the face of established conventions.

To pull a long face : to look dismal.

If something unpleasant happens, you should not pull a long face.

To save face : to avoid humiliation.

We undergo many expenses to save face.

Fall : *To fall on one's feet :* to come out well of a

difficulty; to gain an unexpected good fortune.

It was a hard time when she lost her parents but she fell on her feet.

Fee : *Not worth a pin's fee :* of absolutely no value.

In the face of desperadoes one's life quite often is not worth a pin's fee.

Free : *to make free with :* to take liberties; to be familiar with.

You should not make free with girls at a marriage party.

Fullness : *In the fullness of time :* at the due or destined time.

Every one of us realizes his destiny in the fullness of time.

G

Gather : *Gather oneself together :* to collect all one's powers, like one about to leap.

In an unexpected difficulty, one should gather oneself together.

Good : *To be as good as one's word :* to fulfil one's promise.

You will not do well in life if you are not as good as your word.

Gordian : *To cut the Gordian Knot:* to overcome a

difficulty by violent measures.

One should not go to war and cut the Gordian knot before all other means and measures have been tried out.

Grace : *To take heart of grace :* to take courage from favour shown.

When the king has made you a minister, you can take the heart of grace to become a prime minister.

Grain : *With a grain of salt :* with reservation, as of a story which cannot be believed.

Father heard the news of his son's topping I.F.S. Competition with a grain of salt.

H

Hair : *To make one's hair stand on end :* to give the greatest astonishment or fright to another.

Even a gentle earthquake makes our hair stand on end.

Not to turn a hair : to be undisturbed.

When his son died, Radha Krishan did not turn a hair. What a yogic composure !

Hand : *To catch red-handed :* to catch someone while they are doing something wrong.

The thief was caught red-handed by the police.

Hang : *To hang one's head :* to look sheepish or ashamed.

When an offender is taken to task, he usually hangs his head.

Hang in the balance : to be in doubt or suspense.

In the face of increasing atomic weaponry, the fate of humanity hangs in the balance.

Hare : *To run with the hare and hunt with the hound :* to be on both sides at once.

In the Moscow-Washington conflict, most of the small nations are running with the hare and hunting with the hound.

The police informers run with the hare and hunt with the hound.

Heel : *To show a clean pair of heels :* to run off.

In any serious trouble, many friends do not stand by you but rather show a clean pair of heels.

High : *To hit the high spots :* to go to excess.

When you drink liquor, do not hit the high spots.

Horn : *To make a spoon or spoil a horn :* to attempt something at the risk of failure.

Modern youth will make a spoon or spoil a horn rather than learn from experience.

Put to the horn : to outlaw by three blasts of the bugle.

The recalcitrant member of a criminal society is first put to the horn and then put to death.

To draw in one's borns : to reduce one's enthusiasm.

When an ardent young man fails in his target, he usually draws in the horns.

— I —

Ice : *To break the ice :* to begin work.

For all great enterprises, the Prime Minister is invited to break the ice.

To cut no ice : to count for nothing.

In a company of VIP's, you and I cut no ice.

Ink : *To sling ink :* to write; to earn one's bread by writing; to engage in a controversy.

If you have anything important to say, do not hesitate to sling ink.

I have been slinging ink for the last forty years.

With your superiors it does not pay to sling ink.

Interest : *To make interest for :* to secure favour for.

If you want me to make interest for you, please come to my house.

— J —

Jack : *Jack of all trades :* one who attempts to do

anything.

One who is a jack of all trades is usually a master of none.

Jaw : *To bold one's jaw :* to cease from talking or scolding.

When something goes wrong and cannot be remedied, it is best to hold your jaw.

Joint : *Out of joint :* dislocated; in disorder.

Times are out of joint—*Shakespeare*

To put one's nose out of joint : to supplant in another's love or confidence; to rebuff.

He wanted to romance with her; but she put his nose out of joint.

K

Keep : *To keep body and soul together :* to maintain life.

In these days of high prices, it is hard to keep body and soul together.

To keep one's breath to cool one's porridge : to keep one's peace when further controversy is useless.

In political discussion it is best to keep your breath to cool your porridge.

Key : *To have the key of the street :* to be homeless.

A beggar has the key of the street.

Kirk : *To make a kirk or a mill of it :* do what you please or can with it.

If you feel insulted by my honest advice, you are free to make a kirk or a mill of it.

L

Leg : *Not a leg to stand on :* no case at all.

Don't go to court on trifling matters because you have no leg to stand upon.

Pull one's leg : to make a playful attempt to play upon one's credulity.

If you think I can win the Nobel Prize, you are only pulling my leg.

Light : *According to one's lights :* as far as one's knowledge enables one to judge.

According to my lights, you are accusing a wrong person.

Between two lights : under cover of darkness.

You can find me at home between two lights.

To stand in one's own light : to hinder one's own advantage.

An ungrateful wretch stands in his own light.

Love : *There's no love lost between them* : they have no liking for each other.

There is no point of their getting married as there's no love lost between them.

M

Manner : *To the manner born* : accustomed from birth.

He fished as if to the manner born.

Map : *Off the map* : out of existence; negligible.

My friend is dead and off the map.

The village was bombed off the map.

Medal : *The other side of the medal* : the opposite point of view.

It is best to see the other side of the medal before forming your judgment.

Meet : *Meet halfway* : make concessions in compromise.

If you seek peace, meet your adversary halfway.

Miss : *To miss the bus* : to lose one's opportunity.

He could get a very good job if he had tried but he missed the bus.

Mistake : *And no mistake* : assuredly.

Come, take your great chance, and no mistake.

Mistake one's man : to think lightly of the man one

has to deal with.

If he's going to be your partner, don't mistake your man.

Moon : *To cry for the moon :* to seek something impossible.

His ambition to become a minister is a cry for the moon.

Moonlight flitting : fleeing by night with rent unpaid.

When a tenant is hard up, he is forced to moonlight flitting.

Mountain : *To make a mountain of a molehill :* to exaggerate.

If you have small troubles, don't cry to death, making a mountain of a molehill.

N

Nail : *To hit the nail on the head :* to touch the exact point.

If you call the trader a thug, you hit the nail on the head.

To nail a lie the counter : to prove something wrong as wrong.

In litigation it is not easy to nail a lie to the counter.

Naught : *To set at naught :* To not care about or fear

David was set at naught about Goliath.

Neck : *To get it in the neck :* to be severely dealt with.

When he challenged the king, he got it in the neck.

Neck to neck : exactly equal.

Economics and politics run neck to neck.

To talk through the back of one's neck : to talk wildly, wide of the truth.

When he accused his good friend, he was talking through the back of his neck.

Needle : *To look for a needle in a haystack :* to engage in a hopeless search.

To search for a child in the Kumbh Mela is to look for a needle in a haystack.

Net : *To dance in a net :* to act in imagined concealment.

The woman was very secretive but she was only dancing in a net.

Nick : *In the nick of time :* at the last moment.

The doctor reached the patient in the nick of time.

Out of all nick : out of all reckoning; exceedingly.

The greatness of the Prime Minister is out of all nick.

Nine : *Nine day wonder :* an object of short-lived curiosity.

A marriage is a nine days' wonder.

Nose : *To cut one's nose to spite one's face :* to injure oneself just to spite another.

If you lose a battle, don't cut off your nose to spite your opponents face.

To thrust one's nose into : to meddle officiously with.

Don't thrust your nose into other people's business.

To turn up one's nose at : to receive contemptuously.

If somebody offers you an opportunity, don't turn up your nose at him.

Under one's nose : in full view.

Crime is committed under the nose of the police.

O

Oats : *To sow one's wild oats :* to indulge in youthful excesses.

Young folk are wont to sow their wild oats.

Feel one's oats : to be frisky or assertive.

When a girl is married, she feels her oats.

Oblivion : *To cast into oblivion :* to forget completely.

Dead friends are cast into oblivion.

Oil : *To throw oil on troubled waters :* to pacify a conflict.

In a domestic duel, it is best to throw oil on troubled waters.

To oil one's palm : to bribe.

It is customary to oil officers' palm to get a work done.

Olive **:** *To hold the olive branch :* to seek peace.

When Pakistan lost Bangladesh, Yahya Khan held out the olive branch.

Once : *Once and for all :* once only and never again.

Dame Fortune knocks at your door once and for all.

P

Paper : *Paper tiger :* one needlessly causing fear.

Mao Tse-tung called USA a paper tiger.

Parcel : *Part and parcel :* important portion.

Sovereignty is part and parcel of national independence.

Part : *Parting ways :* fateful decision.

The Congress and Muslim League parted ways in 1947.

Pat : *A pat on the back :* mark of encouragement.

America's reconciliation with China was a pat on the back of Nixon and Kissinger.

Pay : *Pay through the nose :* pay dearly.

For two invasions of India, Pakistan has paid through the nose.

Peel : *Pack and Peel :* to have any dealings.

It not good for you to pack and peel with Manohar Lal.

Peg : *To be a round peg in a square hole :* to be unsuited to the position one occupies.

He got a good job but he was a round peg in a square hole.

Play : *To play fast and loose :* to act in a shifty, inconsistent and reckless fashion.

You must not play fast and loose with your friends.

To play ducks and drakes : to waste foolishly.

You must not play ducks and drakes with your savings.

Plough : *To put one's hand to the plough :* to begin an undertaking.

When you get a contract, waste no time in putting your hand to the plough.

Pound : *To be pennywise and pound foolish :* to save small amounts and waste all.

Old women are pennywise but pound foolish.

Q

Quarter : *At close quarters :* in very near proximity.

They fought at close quarters.

Keep good quarter : keep good watch or order.

The students in the hostel are expected to keep good quarter.

Keep a bad quarter : make a disturbance.

Please don't keep a bad quarter here.

Question : *Out of question :* impossible.

Going home today is out of the question.

Your character is beyond question.

Quiet : *On the quiet :* clandestinely; unobtrusively.

Many things today in India are being done on the quiet.

R

Rack : *To rack one's brains :* to strain one's memory.

I am racking my brains to remember where we met previously.

Rack and ruin : state of neglect and collapse.

Don't let your estate go to rack and ruin.

Ring : *To hold or keep the ring :* to watch a fight and keep others from interfering.

While India and Pakistan fought, Russia held the ring.

Run : *Run together :* mingle and blend.

Good and evil run together in the world.

S

Saddle : *To put the saddle on the right horse :* to impute blame where it is due.

Do not lose your temper and put the saddle on the wrong horse.

Salt : *The salt of the earth :* the choice few of highest excellence.

Enlightened folk are the salt of the earth.

To take with a grain of salt : to believe with some reserve.

The story of a flying saucer has to be taken with a grain of salt.

Say : *To say nothing of :* not to mention.

He earns Rs. 10,000 a month, to say nothing of his wife's salary.

Scorch : *Scorched earth policy :* country devastated before evacuation so as to be useless to an advancing enemy.

Stalin's scorched earth policy defeated Hitler's advancing armies in Russia.

Shake : *To shake the dust from one's feet :* to renounce all intercourse.

In 1947, I shook the dust of Lahore from my feet.

Shirt : *To lose one's Shirt :* to lose one's temper.

Don't lose your shirt over petty matters.

Skeleton : *in the cupboard :* hidden domestic or personal sorrow or shame.

There is a skeleton in every individual's cupboard.

T

Taste : *In good taste :* with intuitive feeling of what is aesthetically or socially right.

Her performance was in good taste.

Terra firma : hard ground; dryland; practicality.

If you look for money in this world, you should stand four square on terra firma.

Throw : *To throw in one's lot :* to join for good or evil.

Japan threw in its lot with Germany in the Second World War.

Toy with : to deal lightly.

Don't toy with your future prospects.

Turn : *To turn round one's little finger :* to be able to persuade to anything.

When he has made up his mind, you cannot turn him round your little finger.

Turn the stomach : nauseate.

The poisonous fruit turned his stomach.

U

Umbrella : *Under the umbrella of :* under the protection of.

Pakistan survives under the umbrella of USA.

V

Vain : *In vain :* fruitlessly.

All his efforts for a reconciliation were in vain.

Veil : *To draw a veil over :* cover, forget.

Let us draw a veil over past differences.

Velvet : *An iron hand in a velvet glove :* a strong policy under courteous dealings.

An iron hand in a velvet glove succeeds better than a velvet hand in an iron glove.

W

Walk : *one's chalks :* to go away without ceremony.

Suddenly he resigned and walked his chalks.

Water : *To make one's mouth water :* to tempt.

Money makes every man's mouth water.

Y

Yeoman's Service : powerful aid.

Italy rendered Germany yeoman's service during the Second World War.

Z

A-to-Z : completely.

He read his books A to Z for the examination.

CHAPTER XI

Words From The Newspapers

Every day newspapers come laden with the ore of good vocabulary; and you can get the gems if only you keep eyes open and a good dictionary alongside to get at the meaning if you fail to pick the sense directly from the context.

Whenever and wherever you learn a new word, do not fail to learn its spelling also, otherwise it cannot be of help in its practical application.

The following pieces are garnered from a single day's newspaper :

ARYABHATTA'S 1500TH ANNIVERSARY

The Prime Minister reminded the nation that "we want scientific thinking to destroy the superstitions which have darkened our lives."

Mrs. Gandhi said, "the *inculcation* of scientific temper is now a part of our duties as citizens. It is not an empty phrase."

Inculcation : giving : imparting. Mrs. Gandhi said : "We want science to light the spark of adventure, to *bestow* the gift of far-reaching vision.

Bestow : confer, give.

She said : "We need a new *breed* of scientist philosophers who can help man in mind, morality and spirit so that *awesome* powers are not used to destroy beyond *redemption* all that has been created in thousands of years."

Breed : class.

Awesome : frightful.

Redemption : salvation; recovery; freedom.

"From a fairly common *perspective,* it is rather well known that nations and civilizations have had a cycle of brilliance and *fade out."*

Perspective : broad study.

Fade-out : dimness.

"The centre of knowledge and learning was in the East for many centuries before moving westward", she said. "In the *resurgence* of Asia and Africa in world affairs since the end of World War II, I hope, as *an optimist,* to see many of the ancient seats of scholarship (which were also the *cradles* of Western Civilization) recapture their old brilliance."

Resurgence : reawakening.

Optimist : one who hopes for the best.

Cradles : nurseries.

DUBIOUS DISTINCTION IN CRIME RECORD

Dubious : doubtful.

Distinction : name and fame.

How can there be distinction in crime ? The word is ironically used. It means "notoriety" here.

SCIENCE FAIR REVEALS STUDENT INGENUITY

Ingenuity : intelligence.

Hundreds of scientific *devices, gadgets and* models created by *budding* scientists were on *display*.....*The* cream of young science *talent* got an *opportunity* to present quality of its *faculties* and its *ingeniousness.* The fair, organized by the Directorate of Education, Delhi Administration, would really prove a *landmark* in science education in Delhi. The fair was *inaugurated* by the Chief Executive Councillor, Mr. Radha Raman. It was a pleasant *coincidence* with the 1500th birth *anniversary* of well-known Indian mathematician, Aryabhata.

Devices : mechanical designs.

Gadgets : small handy machines.

Budding : young, promising.

Display : put on show.

Talent : ability.

Opportunity : chance.

Faculties : abilities.

Ingeniousness : originality, newness.

Landmark : Important point.

Inaugurated : started with ceremony.

Coincidence : happening together

Anniversary : occurring once a year ; happening after a year

HENS KNOW BETTER

Preposterous as it may sound, the UK egg producers' plan to ask their hens to go on strike before Christmas has a thin shell of black humour in it though it sadly lacks the *yolk* of wisdom. One would have thought that, considering the season, the *turkey-hatchers'* association would do that sort of *inane* thing. But one often misjudges. The poultry people want egg prices to be maintained at high level by *eliminating* surpluses. This is the normal nique in certain societies where profits come before hing else. And how are these *eggomaniacs* going to their mad *objective?* By withdrawing the *calcium* hens feed. According to the known rules of *baryard biology,* if there is no calcium *intake* there will be no egg-laying. And if there is no laying, the poultry farmers will be *clucking* with joy at the *shekels* they *rake* in. Not that such ugly tricks have not been played before. A *bumper* harvest in a South American Country once led to the burning of millions of *bushels* of wheat. Western Europe has seen milk and wine being *splashed* on the streets in vast quantities. Tomatoes, potatoes, and cabbages grown with great human effort have been *likewise* destroyed in order to *establish* the *sovereignty* of profits. *Antibiotics* are added to *livestock* feed so that the animals will grow fatter sooner (meaning more money quicker). All this is done if many lands and few people seem to mind the *gross absurdity* of it. But in this egg case the plan may not quite work out. Many of these birds are more intelligent than their owners though their five-gram brain is *chickenfeed* when compared to a human brain which weighs some 1,300 grams. When the hens can't get the calcium, they are sure to turn to plain mud which is rich in the *mineral.* Then what will men do ? *Smash* all the surplus eggs and make an *omelette* as large as Britain ?

Preposterous : foolish.

Yolk : the yellow part of egg.

Turkey-hatchers : producers of turkey fowls.

Inane : foolish.

Eliminating : removing.

Eggomaniacs : people who are mad after eggs.

Objective : purpose.

Calcium : lime.

Barnyard biology : life of poultry fowls.

Intake : element in food.

Shekels : coins, money.

Rake : earn quickly.

Clucking : sound of hens.

Bumper : big.

Bushels : Large Quantities of wheat.

Splashed : thrown as water.

Likewise : similarly.

Establish : make.

Sovereignty : complete power.

Antibiotics : medicine for killing bacteria.

Livestock : animals kept in captivity for use of their products.

Gross absurdity : total foolishness.

Chickenfeed : very small.

Mineral : salt, calcium.

Smash : break.

Omelette : a dish made of eggs.

KNEW HIS RIGHTS

The *prosecuting attorney* looked *severely* at the small red-faced man who had been *summoned* into court and who returned his *gaze flinching.*

"So you kicked your landlord downstairs?" *queried* the attorney. "Did you imagine that was within the rights of the *tenant?*"

"I'll bring my lease in and show it to you," said the little man, growing redder, "and I'll *wager* you'll agree with me that anything they've forgotten to *prohibit* in the *lease,* I had a right to do the very first chance I got."

Prosecuting attorney : government lawyer appearing for complainant in a crime case.

Severely : sternly.

Summoned : ordered to appear before the court.

Flinching : fearfully.

Queried : questioned.

Tenant : one who rents a house.

Wager : bet.

Prohibit : prevent.

Lease : rent deed.

CHAPTER XII

Spellings

When you learn a new word, it is important that you also learn its spelling at the same time. To spell a word wrongly is a literary disaster and reflects very badly on your reputation.

It is better not to know a word than to know a word and not be acquainted with its spelling. When you do not know the spelling of a word, it is better not to use it at all. You can substitute it with a word whose spelling you are fully aware of.

To learn the spelling of a big word, it is best to break it up into parts whose spellings are easy to grasp and remember. There are three things of importance concerning every new word which you add to the treasury of your vocabulary :

i. Spelling of the word.

ii. Meaning of the word.

iii. Usage of the word in a sentence form.

The following words are specially selected for your comprehension in all its three components :

1. **Aphaeresis** (a-phae-re-sis)

   The taking away of a letter or syllable at the beginning of a word.

   "Merica" is an aphaeresis of "America".

   "Morning" is an aphaeresis of "Good morning."

2. **Apophthegm** (a-poph-the-gm)

   Terse saying, pithy maxim.

   Madame Blavatsky's *Voice of Silence* is a compilation of Vedic apophthegms.

3. **Aposiopesis** (apo-sio-pe-sis)

   Sudden breaking-off in speech.

   Hitler dramatized aposiopesis in public addresses.

4. **Autocephalous** (auto-ce-phalous)

   Having its own head; independent.

   A public undertaking is an autocephalous organization.

5. **Avant-Garde** (avant-garde)

   The pioneers or innovators in any art or particular period.

   Swadeshi Movement was the *avant garde* of Indian Independence.

6. **Belvedere** (bel-ve-dere)

open-sided gallery to view scenery from, usually at roof top level

Kutab Minar is an excellent belvedere.

7. **Bonhomie** (bon-ho-mie)

Geniality.

The party was characterised by bonhomie.

8. **Contravention** (con-tra-ven-tion)

Infringement.

Do nothing in contravention of high moral principles.

9. **Criterion** (cri-ter-ion)

Principle, standard.

What is the criterion of the "poor" for doles ?

10. **Ecclesiastical** (ecc-le-siast-i-cal.)

Of the church or clergy; religious.

The State should not interfere in ecclesiastical affairs.

11. **Entrepreneur** (entre-pre-neur)

A person who undertakes an enterprise or business, with the chance of profit or loss.

Quick technological development calls for young entrepreneurs.

12. **Epicurean** (epi-cur-ean)

One devoted to the pleasure of refined sensuous enjoyments.

He was positively epicurean in his lifestyle.

13. **Eventuality** (even-tu-al-ity)

Possible event.

Your true friends will stand by you in any eventuality.

14. **Excommunicate** (ex-comm-uni-cate)

Officially exclude from a religion.

The morally corrupt should be excommunicated.

15. **Gibberish** (gib-ber-ish)

Unintelligible speech; meaningless sounds.

Politicians stuff their mighty pronouncements with sheer gibberish.

16. **Haecceity** (hae-cce-ity)

The quality of a thing that makes it describable as 'this' one.

Everything and everybody enjoys a certain amount of haecceity.

17. **Horticulture** (hort-i-culture)

The art of garden cultivation.

Horticulture should be popularized as a hobby.

18. **Hortus Siccus** (Arranged collection of dried plants; collection of uninteresting facts.)

A government statistical document is a *hortus siccus.*

19. **Indestructible**

    Not destructible by dissolution of parts.

    Both Soul and Matter are indestructible.

20. **Lixiviate**

    Separate into soluble and insoluble constituents by percolation of water.

    Sand and sugar can be lixiviated.

21. **Marmalade**

    Preserve of citrus fruits.

    Would you like jam or marmalade with the toast?

22. **Monochrome** (mo-no-chrome)

    A photograph or picture executed in one colour or in different tints of one colour.

    A monochrome painting is very soothing to the soul.

23. **Neologism** (neo-lo-gism)

    Coining or using of new words; a new-coined word.

    Great writing is seldom full of neologisms.

24. **Neophyte** (neo-phy-te)

    Novice; beginner.

    Neophytes undergo severe tests.

25. **Oxytone** (ox-y-tone)

Words with acute accent on the last syllable.

Tamil language is highly oxytoned.

26. **Penumbra** (pen-um-bra)

Partial shadow.

The Cabinet stands in the penumbra of the Prime Minister.

27. **Quinquagenarian**

Fifty years old.

Quinquagenarians are in power everywhere.

28. **Rumbustious**

Boisterous, uproarious.

It was a rumbustious gathering in the club.

29. **Skedaddle** (ske-dad-dle)

To run away;

When the police came on the scene, the hooligans skedaddled.

CHAPTER XII

Synonyms and Antonyms

Synonyms mean words of the same meaning. Antonyms mean words of the opposite meaning. "Brilliant" is a synonym of the word "bright" but "dark" is an antonym of the word "bright".

These synonyms and antonyms are important, because you need not repeat the same word again and again. You can use another word expressing the same meaning.

Every word in the dictionary has its own synonyms and antonyms. Some words of current use are enlisted here to spice up your writing and speech.

Abbreviate

Synonyms	*Antonyms*	*Synonyms*	*Antonyms*
Abridge	Extend	Digest	Elongate
Condense	Stretch out	Curtail	Prolong

Shorten	Lengthen	Contract	Protract

Abstemious

Synonyms	*Antonyms*	*Synonyms*	*Antonyms*
Temperate	Intoxicated	Easy	High
Abstinent	Tipsy	Tempered	Elevated
Sober	Drunk	Reasonable	Maudlin
Tame	Wild	Tolerant	Inebriate

Accelerate

Synonyms	*Antonyms*	*Synonyms*	*Antonyms*
Hasten	Slow down	Gain	Lose
Expedite	Procrastinate	Ground	Dangle
Quicken	Slacken		

Beauty

Synonyms	*Antonyms*	*Synonyms*	*Antonyms*
Loveliness	Ugliness	Houri	Witch
Gorgeousness	Loathesomeness	Adonis	Gargoyle
Attractiveness	Disfigurement	Enchantress	Spectre
Elegance	Inelegance	Charmer	Caliban
Comeliness	Homeliness	Glory	Scarecrow
Refinement	Sordidness	Venus	Satyr

Inauguration

Synonyms	*Antonyms*	*Synonyms*	*Antonyms*
Beginning	End	Kick off	Tail end
Introduction	Conclusion	Curtain raiser	Final Curtain
Outset	Termination	Infancy	Quietus
Alpha	Omega	Birth	Death
Embarkation	Disembarkation		

Precious

Synonyms	*Antonyms*	*Synonyms*	*Antonyms*
Dear	Cheap	Inestimable	Petty
Superior	Inferior	Invaluable	Valueless
Worthy	Worthless	Lovable	Despicable
Expensive	Low-priced	Attractive	Repulsive

Education

Synonyms	*Antonyms*	*Synonyms*	*Antonyms*
Knowledge	Ignorance	Prudence	Stupidity
Literacy	Illiteracy	Wisdom	Foolishness
Development	Degeneration		

Effeminate

Synonyms	*Antonyms*	*Synonyms*	*Antonyms*
Womanly	Manly	Fragile	Venile

Womanish	Mannish	Emasculate	Robust
Feminine	Masculine	Soft	Hard
She-man	He-man	Sissy	Tomboy

Naked

Synonyms	*Antonyms*	*Synonyms*	*Antonyms*
Naked	Clothed	Explicit	Implicit
Uncovered	Covered	Open	Hidden
Nude	Draped	Revealed	Concealed
Stripped	Robed		

Nincompoop

Synonyms	*Antonyms*	*Synonyms*	*Antonyms*
Nitwit	Wit	Jolterhead	Judge
Fool	Philosopher	Block	Doctor
Numbskull	Connoisseur	Inexperienced	Expert
Spoony	Sophist		

CHAPTER XIV

Homonyms

Homonyms are words which are characterised by the same sound, but have different spellings, and also different meanings.

Ail and Ale

Ail : pain, trouble, illness.

Ale : drink.

What ails you?

Will you have a cup of ale?

Ait, ate and eight

Ait : an island.

Ate : past tense of "to eat".

Eight : 8.

They ate their food on the ait.

They ate eight mangoes on the ait.

Altar and alter

Altar: platform for worship.

Alter: change.

The devout do not alter their form of worship on the altar.

Annalize and Analyze

Annalize : to record.

Analyze : to break up into parts.

Firdausi annalized the history of Iran.

Please analyze this sentence.

Aisle, I'll and Isle

Aisle: passage between 2 rows of seats.

I'll : I will.

I'll meet you in the aisle.

Isle : Island.

All and Awl

All : everyone.

Awl : an instrument in shoemaking.

All shoes are made with an awl.

Aloud and allowed

Aloud : in high tone.

Allowed : permitted.

Nobody is allowed to sing aloud in this room.

Ante and anti

Ante : before.

Anti : opposed.

The man who lives in the ante room seems to be anti-communist.

Arc and ark

Arc : part of a circle.

Ark : boat.

Noah's ark moved in an arc.

Ascent and Assent

Ascent : climb.

Assent : consent.

Nanda Devi assented to climb Nanda Devi and died on the ascent.

Aught and ought

Aught : anything.

Ought : should.

Have you aught that you ought to keep to yourself?

Awed and Odd

Awed : dreaded.

Odd : uneven.

The odd happenings awed the guests.

Artist and Artiste

Artist : painter.

Artiste : dancer.

This picture has been made by an artist.

Many artistes work in this film.

Bait and Bate

Bait : food to allure.

Bate : to lessen; reduced.

He baited a fish when his food was bated.

Bark and Barque

Bark : the cry of a dog.

Barque : a vessel.

A dog barked when they entered the barque.

Bite and Bight

Bite: cut through with teeth.

Bight: Curve in coastline.

Ball and bawl

Ball : round body, dance.

Bawl : to cry aloud.

The child bawled when his ball was lost.

Bard and barred

Bard : poet.

Barred : fastened with a bar.

The bard found that the door was barred.

Baron and barren

Baron : nobleman.

Barren : unfruitful; childless.

The baron has a barren wife.

Boarder and border

Boarder : lodger.

Border : margin.

Are you a boarder in Miranda House?

He lives on the border.

Berth and birth

Berth : sleeping place in a train, ship, etc.

Birth : being born.

The child's birth took place on the berth, on the way from Mumbai to Delhi.

CHAPTER XV

Rhyming Words

It is common characteristic of Punjabi language to have double words which spice colloquialism, such as *Roti-shoti* (bread or something), *Pani Shani* (water or some other drink), *Shadi-shoodi*(marriage or some other similar affair), *dost-wost* (friend or some other acquaintance), etc.

Such double words are not frequent in the English language. There are some such rare combinations which should be learnt to salt and spice your expressions. Some of these expressions in common use are the following:—

Rag-Tag : rabble, unorganised

Keep clear of the rag-tag in the college corridors.

Hotch-Potch : medley; mixture.

The dinner was a hotch-potch of Indian and Chinese food.

Hodge-Podge : medley; mixture.

The function was a hodge-podge of rites and riutals.

Hurly-Burly : tumult; confusion.

He found all the hurly-burly tiresome.

Mumbo-Jumbo : meaningless senseless.

There is much mumbo-jumbo in every religion.

Hustle-Bustle : fun; show; crowdedness; activity.

A marriage function is full of hustle-bustle.

Roly-Poly : fat, round, podgy.

The shopkeeper is quite roly-poly.

Walkie-Talkie : a portable wireless transmitting set.

The constable contacted the police headquarters on the walkie-talkie.

Hubbub : riot; a confused sound of many voices, great confusion or noise created in a particular situation.

There was an increasing hubbub from the great reception hall below.

He would have been pardoned long ago if it hadn't been for the hubbub created by the media.

Hubble-Bubble : bubbling sound; *hookah;* confusion.

I avoid hubble-bubble functions.

He smoked a hubble-bubble.

Hocus-pocus : a trick to confuse someone.

There's been a bit of hocus pocus going on here.

Powwow : to confer; conference.

They powwowed for peace.

It was a noisy powwow.

Kowtow : to kneel.

I will not kowtow to a king.

Lowbrow : common; not intellectual.

It was a lowbrow gathering.

Helter-Skelter : in confusion.

The students ran helter-skelter in the campus.

Bigwig : important people.

People kowtow to bigwigs for favours.

Razzle-Dazzle : rowdy frolic.

Children are fond of razzle-dazzle.

CHAPTER XVI

Foreign Phrases

These words and phrases, from Latin, Greek and modern foreign languages, are more or less in common use in English language and literature.

These are useful in highbrow writings and critical appreciations of poetry, drama, art or sculpture, politics and sociology.

These are of no value, while dealing with people who are semi-literate, and you are not expected, as Jesus Christ said, "to throw pearls before the swine."

A Bas (French): down, down with !

A Beneplacito (Italian): at pleasure.

Ab Imo Pectore (Latin) : from the bottom of my heart.

Ab Initio (Latin) : from the beginning.

A Bon Chat, Bon Rat (French) : to a good cat a good rat; well-matched; set a thief to catch a thief.

Actum Est De Republica (Latin): it is all up with the state.

Actum Ne Agas (Latin) : do not do what is already done.

A demi (French): by halves.

Ad Finem (Latin) : to the end.

Ad Infinitum (Latin) : to infinity.

Ad Vitam Aut Culpam (Latin) : for life or till some misconduct is proved.

Affaire D' Amour (French) : a love affair.

Affaire De Coeur (French) : an affair of the heart.

Affaire de Honneur (French): an affair of honour.

Agent Provocateur (French): one employed to lead others by pretended sympathy into acts of incurring penalties.

Aide-Memoire (French) : an aid to memory.

Aigre-Doux (French) : bitter-sweet.

A La (French): in the manner of.

Albricias (Spanish): a reward to the bearer of good news.

Album Graecum (Latin) : the dried dung of dogs, once used for inflammation of the throat.

Alcaiceria (Spanish): a bazaar.

Alexipharmakon (Greek) : an antidote, counter-poison.

La Ilaba llla 'Llab (Arabic) : There is no God but the God.

Altum Silentium (Latin) : profound silence.

Anak (Hebrew): a race of giants.

Anonyma (Latinized Greek): a showy woman of light fame, whom one is not supposed to know.

Ardentia verba (Latin): words that burn, glowing language.

Aufklarung (German): enlightenment.

Auf Wiedecshen (German): Good bye till we meet again.

Autobahn (German): an arterial double road for motor traffic only.

Bacchus (Latin), *Bakchos* (Greek): God of wine.

Beatae Memoriae **:** for the blessed memory.

Beati Pacifici (Latin): Blessed are the peacemakers.

Bella, Horrida Bella (Latin): wars, horrid wars.

Caesar Non Supra Grammaticos (Latin): Caesar has no authority over the grammarians.

Celui Qui Veut, Peut (French): who can will.

Ce Monde Est Plein De Fous (French): this world is full of madmen.

Danke Schon (German) : Many thanks.

De Luxe (French): sumptuous.

Detente (French): relaxation of strained relations.

Edition De luxe (French): a splendid and expensive edition of a book.

Ex Nilo Nil Fit (Latin): out of nothing nothing comes.

Facta Non Verba (Latin): deeds, not words.

Factum Est (Latin): it is done.

Gnothi Seauton (German): know thyself.

Hora Fugit (Latin): the hour flies.

Ich Dien (German): I serve.

Idee Fixe (French): a fixed idea, monomania.

Jacta Est Alea (Latin): the die is cast.

Laus Deo (Latin): praise to God.

Macte Virtute Esto (Latin): go on in your virtue.

Ne Plus Ultra (Latin): nothing further; the uttermost point or extreme perfection of anything.

Obscurum per Obscurius (Latin): explaining the obscure by means of the more obscure.

Quo Vadis? (Latin): Whither goest thou?

CHAPTER XVII

Word-Building Exercises 1

Choose the right word from the alternatives given to fill in the blank :

1. A mackintosh is a ____________ material made of rubber and cloth for garments.

   (thin, water-proof, thick)

2. An ostrich is a large ____________ African and Arabian bird.

   (slow-moving, swift-running)

3. An oublette is a secret ____________ with entrance only by trapdoor.

   (palace, fort, dungeon)

4. Pueperal means of, due to ____________.

   (disease, old age, child birth)

5. A Seville orange is a bitter orange used for

_________ (pickle, jam, marmalade)

6. A versatile person is one who readily turns from one subject or _____________ to another. (place, occupation, shop)

7. Recriminate means to retort with an _____________ or indulge in counter charges. (joke, accusation, request)

8. Subterfuge is an attempt to escape _____________ or defeat in argument by evading the issue. (punishment, censure, loss, fine)

9. Succedaneum is a _____________ thing that one falls back on in default of another. (substitute, better, worse)

10. A trellis is a _____________ of light wooden crossbars nailed together. (network, lattice, fabric)

11. A Scupper is a _____________ in a ship's side to carry off water from deck. (drain, sewage, hole)

Answers to above

1. Waterproof
2. Swift-running
3. Dungeon
4. Childbirth
5. Marmalade
6. Occupation
7. Accusation
8. Censure
9. Substitute
10. Lattice
11. Hole

CHAPTER XVIII

Word-Building Exercises 2

Here, different meanings have been given against some selected words. Tick the word which you believe to be the nearest in meaning.

1. **Pugnacious**
    A. Troublesome
    B. Comfortable
    C. Stubborn
    D. Truculent
    E. Persistent
2. **Scavenger**
    A. Messenger
    B. Street cleaner
    C. Gentleman

D. Politician

E. Secretary

3. Cynosure

A. Centre of attention

B. Centre of darkness

C. Obscurity

D. Certainty

E. Change

4. Oscillate

1. To kiss
2. Swing back and forth
3. To bind fast
4. To change horses
5. To enrapture

5. Cynicism

A. Socialism

B. Sneering disbelief

C. Atheism

D. Philanthropy

E. Strictness

6. Catapult

A. To shoot

B. Young one of a cat.

C. To hurl
D. Jump
E. Live forever

7. Remorse

A. Pity
B. Haughtiness
C. Vengeance
D. Self-reproach
E. Punishment

8. Parasite

A. National anthem
B. National emblem
C. Coward
D. Hanger-on
E. Lover

9. Crucial

1. Comic
2. Tragic
3. Critical and decisive
4. Persistent
5. Mortal

10. Tirade

A. Reconciliation.

B. Forethought

C. Pessimism.

D. Playfulness

E. Long angry speech

Answers to above

1. **Pugnacious** (pug nay shus)

Truculent; ready to fight, from the Latin word *Pugnus* (first). Pugnacious politician.

2. **Scavenger** (skav in jer)

Street cleaner. The word is from the Anglo-Norman word *Scawager* (toll collector who was also required to keep streets clean). It also means an animal eating decayed matter.

The vulture is a scavenger of nature.

3. **Cynosure** (sy no sure)

Centre of interest. From Latin *cynosure* (the constellation Ursa Minor, containing the Pole Star which guided ancient navigators).

4. **Oscillate** (oss i late).

To swing back and forth. It is from Latin *oscillare,* from *oscillum,* a small mark of Bacchus, hung from tree, especially in vineyards, so as to be moved easily by the wind.

Life oscillates between hope and despair.

5. **Cynicism** (sin' is iz'm)

Sneering disbelief. Scepticism. The cynics were a group of philosophers in ancient Greece. From Greek kunikos (doglike or churlish).

Modern youth is overcome with cynicism.

6. **Catapult** (kat a pult)

To hurl. Latin *catapulta* means instrument for throwing arrows and rocks.

The city of Troy was catapulted for destruction.

The earthquake catapulted the houses.

7. **Remorse** (ri mors)

Self-reproach; anguish caused by guilt. Latin *remordere* from *re* (again) and *mordere* (to bite).

After killing his friend, he suffered from terrible remorse.

After telling a lie to his father, Mahatma Gandhi was overcome with remorse.

8. **Parasite** (par'a site).

Hanger-on. One organism living off another. From Greek *parasitos* (one who eats at the table of another).

Every institution is full of parasites.

9. **Crucial** (crew'sh'l)

Critical and decisive. From Latin *crux* (cross)

Elections are crucial in politics.

10. **Tirade** (tie' rade).

Long angry speech. Literally, a volley of words. From Italian *tirata* (volley of firearms).

The opposition launched a tirade against the Prime Minister.

Radiant Health Series

1. *Parvesh Handa*
   Skin Care
2. *Parvesh Handa*
   Breast Care
3. *Dr. Vinod Verma*
   Yoga 9 Week Course
4. *Swami Akshaya Atmanand*
   Yogic Asanas and Pranayama
5. *W. H. Bates, M.D.*
   Better Eyesight Without Glasses
6. *Dr. M. S. Agarwal*
   The Complete Book of Eye Care
7. *Dr. Mohan Lal Kathotia*
   Surya Chikitsa : Colour Therapy for Common Diseases (Illustrated)
8. *Chho Dev*
   Beauty and Body Book (Illustrated)
9. *Astrid Goosmann-Legger*
   Acupressure Therapy (Illustrated)
10. *James C. Thomson*
    Heart Disease - Preventing & Cure
11. *Phyllis Speight*
    Overcoming Rheumatism & Arthritis (Illustrated)
12. *Dr. M. T. Santwani*
    Magneto Theraphy for Common Diseases (Illustrated)
13. *Dr. Inderjit K. Bharthakur*
    Choose The Sex of Your Child
14. *Dr. Lakshminarain Sharma*
    (Illustrated) Includes Asana Chart
15. *Dr. O.P. Jaggi*
    Health Care for Plus Fifty